Restless Spirit
A Tipsy Fairy Tale

E. Chris Garrison

Chapter One

Their eyes scanned me from head to toe and back up again. Annabelle whistled. All of Phil's visible skin turned pink, and his eyes returned for a second scan.

"Holy crap, Skye, is that even *legal*?" said Annabelle, her eyes shifting from side to side as if looking for police roaming the Big Con dealer room. I winked and blew her a kiss, vamping it up. She licked her lips and laughed.

A sort of whine escaped Phil. Annabelle and I turned to look at him, and he forced a smile, mopping sweat from his brow with one of the souvenir Fantasy Free Form bandannas from the table. He held up his cell phone and asked, "May I?"

I put a hand on my hip and posed. "Why else am I wearing this? Go for it."

Phil's phone made several beeps as he took pictures.

"Let me see?" I said.

He held up the phone for me to see. The image cut off the top of my head and my legs below my kneecaps. In between, I saw my own smiling face, fire truck red lipstick outlining my cat-that-ate-the-canary grin, eyes peering through dishwater blond swoop bangs. Below my face? Well, a lot of my skin showed.

My costume, commissioned by FFF, but made by my dear friend Leslie, was a vision in gold and cream. Gold cupped my breasts; gold lined the silk folds of the skirt that swished only halfway down my thighs. A gilded toy sword swung on a gold sequined belt on my hips. The only thing spoiling the fantasy image was my Big Con badge, which read "Skye MacLeod / FFF Vendor." I giggled with glee. "Oh Annabelle, your girlfriend is a booth babe!"

"Best. Con. Ever." said Phil, taking his phone back. He poked at the screen. I'm sure I was moments away from being posted on the FFF Facebook page.

Annabelle tsked. "Really, Skye?"

I slid up to Annabelle, put my hands behind her neck and pulled myself in close, nose to nose with her. "Are you saying you don't like how I look?"

Annabelle gave me a raspberry, wet at this range. "I love it. I just don't like the herd of nerds ogling you for the next few days."

I gave her a peck on the lips and let her go. "Sweetie, it's a job, and it pays better than the last few."

She broke eye contact with me, eyes scanning around the vendor hall. "Yeah, I know. It's not the money, Skye, it's…"

"No," I said. "Not here, not now, not in front of Phil, okay?"

Phil turned a deeper pink and stood up with a grunt. He wandered a few feet away, pretending to inspect the booth.

It was Annabelle's turn to redden. "I wasn't. I mean, okay, I started. Sorry. This is just a temporary gig though…"

"Please, just stop. I'm working on it, okay, hon?"

She met my eyes and nodded. "Yeah. Look. The guy at the door told me I couldn't stay here without a badge, I gotta go. I'm working tonight anyway. Text me?"

I took in a deep breath and let it out. "I will."

She put her arms around my waist, clasped them in the small of my back, and stood on tiptoes to give me a deeper kiss. "The nerds can look all they want, but no touching, right?"

"Oh no. No no no. That's *your* job."

She smiled, let go, and walked away with a wave. I watched her go.

"I don't feel so bad now," said Phil, from right behind me. "Huh?"

"I mean, if I had to choose between me and her? That's a no-brainer."

I turned to look at Phil. His eyes followed my girlfriend as she swaggered out of the hall.

"Aw, Phil, don't be like that. You know I adore you."

"Yeah, yeah, I know." The big guy sighed, eyes lowered. "And, Skye?"

I nodded. "Yeah?"

"Thanks for signing on. I think Fantasy Free Form is about to have a population explosion, with you on board."

I laughed. "It's a great costume, but I'm still the same gawky Skye."

He frowned. "You're not talking crap about my friend Skye, are you?"

"Nothing wrong with gawky, is there? I'm just saying I'm as big a nerd as you or any of the others at Big Con. I've been *dying* to go for years, ever since I moved to Indy, but I couldn't afford it. Now I've got a four day pass and I'm being *paid* to be here, so even Annabelle can't object."

"She's not happy about all this?"

I shrugged. "She's glad I've got something. The money from my last job with Rebecca has just about run out, and it's been a month since I've had anything. Even Heath hasn't called me for brewery duty."

"Why's that, Skye? You're bright, and capable and charismatic…"

What could I tell him? Rebecca Burton only hired me for the occasional paranormal investigation as a consultant because of my second sight. That power only works well when I've had a drink or three. I'd hopped on the wagon for the Bloomington job to impress her, and because it hadn't involved anything otherworldly. Well, it'd involved cultists and the cyberspace game world of Fantasy Free Form, but not the fairy world my talent let me see.

Phil though, he was a friend. He'd been protective of me when we'd gotten sucked quite literally into his game world. Not that I really needed protecting. My avatar there had been a bad-ass warrior woman, with much more substantial armor and armament than this sexed up costume. But he'd had a little crush on me, and was brave enough to admit it. That endeared him to me, whether as the white bearded wizard he'd become in the game world, or the over-sized teddy bear he was in real life. The memory of having to let him down easy, because of Annabelle, made me wistful.

Phil prompted me again. "Skye? What's wrong? Something you want to tell me?"

So, the truth. "Phil, I've been fired for drinking on the job more times than I can count in the past year."

His mouth made an "O" of surprise. "I… I mean… Gosh, Skye…"

I held up a hand. "I have a reason for it, but it's easily as crazy as what we went through when we became our characters in FFF. Crazier."

He laughed. "Go on."

I smiled. "So, I'll skip my origin story, but I have a superpower. A little one."

Phil raised an eyebrow.

"Well, so, if I drink, I can see fairies."

"Now you're just making fun of me," he said, and I was surprised at the hint of a whine in his voice, his eyes cast downward.

I put a hand on his shoulder and gave him a quick squeeze. "No, Phil, I'm not joking. Alcohol activates my second sight. And it gets weirder."

He looked up at me, lips pressed into a tight line, but his eyes were curious.

"Once upon a time, I lost a little bit of my soul. It leaked out. That bit of me, well, it became its own little person. Guess you can't have part of a soul. It just becomes another soul. Like if you take a lump of clay, and split it into two lumps, those aren't half a lump each, they're just smaller lumps. You know?"

He nodded, waiting.

"So anyway, yeah. The smaller lump of my soul, it's this little version of me, I call her Minnie. I can't see her unless I'm tipsy, either."

Phil snorted. "Minnie? Like the mouse?"

I shrugged. "More like Dr. Evil's Mini Me."

He laughed. "That bad?"

I shook my head. "No, Minnie's awesome. She's adorable and feisty and really smart."

"Like you," he said.

My turn to snort. "You're awfully sweet. Nah, Minnie's become her own thing, even if she came from me. We're like sisters. Except she's in that fairy world all the time and I'm in this world."

My cell phone ringing interrupted Phil's reply. The Mission: Impossible theme made me cheer out loud with delight; that meant it was the one person I'd been dying to hear from.

I answered, "Hey there, bosslady! What's going on?"

"Skye, are you alone? Don't say my name out loud if you're not." Rebecca Burton's voice was like an angel's to my ears. This could mean another paying job!

"Uhm, no, not really, I'm helping Phil set up at Big Con."

Phil groaned to his feet and meandered around the nearby booths once more.

"Are you? What an interesting coincidence. If you weren't already there, I'd ask you to go. Hmm. I need an agent to keep a lookout in the downtown Indy area, there's been, well, you might say a 'disturbance in the Force,' so to speak." I couldn't help but smile at her formal attempt at geekery.

"Sure thing. Usual rates?" *Cha-ching! Double paychecks!*

"Hmm, yes. No hazard pay at this time, you are just there to observe, not to engage, whatever happens. Understand me, Skye?" I heard some kind of growling, groaning noise, far off in the background on her end of the line. Was it a coyote?

"Mmmhmm, I gotcha. So, what am I looking for?"

Rebecca paused. "I'm not exactly sure, yet. I'm getting mixed reports, but if any of them are to be believed, something big is coming." Barking and scuffling came from the phone, closer now.

"So, like, from the fairy realm?" I said.

"Some sort of spirit activity, that's all that these reports have in common." I knew from her tone that Rebecca wasn't happy she didn't know more. She preferred to be the one with secrets. "Be sure to check around outside the convention center and other places downtown, Skye. I have my doubts that a major disturbance would happen where there are crowds. You and I know spirits prefer to operate in the shadows and remote areas."

"Yep. Okay, sure thing, I'll see what I can see. You know what that means, right?"

Rebecca sighed. "Yes, I realize that it means alcohol will be involved. Try to keep it to the bare minimum. You're trouble enough sober."

"I can't operate blind, and I'm worth two Skyes if I can talk to Minnie. She's got her own connections on the other side, you know?"

"Very well. Just be careful, and report anything you find out back to me. Call me or use the encrypted messaging app. If you get in trouble, get out to report, it's more important that we know what's going on so we can engage properly later."

"Gotcha. Will you be joining me?"

A forlorn howl came from my phone's speaker. "No. I'm otherwise occupied right now. A bit messy, if you understand. But if things escalate there, I'll do what I can to get other agents or get there as quickly as possible."

I got my courage up and said, "Boss? I'm a little short on funds, so any advance you might be able to provide?"

"Yes, of course, I'll have it arranged; you'll find your retainer fee in your account by close of business today."

I bit my lip to keep from cheering in Rebecca's ear.

After a pause, she said, "Anything else? The mess is getting messier here." I heard her cover the mic and shout something.

"Are you okay?"

Rebecca's voice rose in pitch just a bit and she said, "Fine, Skye. I have to go now."

"Take care!" I said.

She hung up, cutting off an animal's snarl.

Damn. I wonder what she's up against.

Before shutting off my phone, I checked its battery. It read 88%. I've learned a trick or two from my ghost hunting friends; some kinds of spirits drain batteries by their presence. It was actually a pretty good charge, considering it was almost lunchtime.

I turned to look for Phil, and found him talking to a tall, pale, gaunt man dressed in black jeans and a black Twilight: Breaking Dawn t-shirt. I groaned out loud before I could stop myself. The boys turned, and I crossed my arms as they both scanned me up and down again.

"Hi there, Ernie," I said.

He stopped scanning me, and though he's as tall as I am, his eyes focused somewhere below my chin as he said, "Dang it, Skye, this is a convention. Call me by my title."

"Don't whine, O Night Duke, it doesn't become you. But I'm working here, I'm not in game."

"Well, I was hoping for some game time from you. You know about the plans our Duchy has for Big Con, I'm going to need some help. My *wife*."

Phil's eyes darted between Ernie's face and mine.

I answered Phil's look before Ernie could go on. "It's a live-action role-playing game, Phil. We're married in-game *only*. For political purposes."

Ernie grinned.

Phil almost pouted, but nodded. "I think I'm playing the wrong game."

I laughed. "Don't let your customers hear you say that."

Ernie said, "Skye, do you think you'll have game time later? Con starts tomorrow, and we've got to be ready."

I shrugged. "Real life comes first, I gotta pay the bills. But sure, I can meet you at Heath's around, say, four-ish?"

He smiled.

"I gotta get back to work," I said, catching Phil's eye.

Phil nodded. "Yeah, we have to get set up, we're behind."

Ernie shrugged. "Anyway, I have something else to talk to you about. Something weird. Tell you later, but it's pretty freaky."

"How freaky, O Night Duke?" I knew this was just a ploy to hang around me in my sexy costume a few minutes longer, but Rebecca did say to be on the lookout.

"Okay, Skye," Ernie said, tone turning serious. He looked me in the eyes for the first time that day and said, "Your boyfriend's ghost came to visit me last night, and he's pissed."

The room spun around me and I felt much too lightheaded. It's a good thing Phil was standing near enough to grab onto, or I might have landed on the floor on my ass.

No, it turned out to be a concert. The street had been blocked off, and some band dressed in Star Trek uniforms played rock music to dancing con-goers. My run slowed almost to a halt, and I had to squeeze through the wall of dancing fans.

"Bonk bonk! Bonk bonk on the head!" they cried, pumping fists in the air to the catchy lyrics.

Ahhhh, my people! Even in my frustration prying my way through, I felt the warmth of kinship in this crowd. Most would get my corny jokes and Doctor Who references.

I passed from the rock show crowd and into another cluster of people. Everyone carried cups of beer, it seemed. The aroma was heavenly; it smelled so familiar.

Then I saw the banner. Heath's Heather Honey Gruit had been brewed up as the official beer of the convention.

The same beer King Bask, the fairy Transit King, had suggested to him. The one that worked to enhance my "talent" to allow me to see auras, too.

I recognized some of his brewing crew supervising samples being handed out. Heath's a friend, and he'd confided his plans to make his brewpub *the* place to be for Big Con.

I collided with someone taller than me. I grabbed onto him so neither of us would fall down, and found myself nose to chin with none other than Greg Heath himself. Something cold and wet trickled down my back.

I let go and felt my cheeks warm. "I'm so sorry, Greg, I didn't see you there!"

He tapped his beakish nose and said, "You didn't see this schnoz? Right. I think you did that on purpose, Skye." Heath smiled.

"No, I really was just… I mean I have a date… I mean, NOT a date, totally not…"

He held out a three quarters full plastic cup of amber colored beer. "Hush. First one's on the house." He shrugged. "Spilled the rest on you."

I took the cup from him as we laughed together. I took a breath and let it out.

"Well?" he pointed at the cup with a jut of his pointed chin.

"Oh!" I took a long drink of the sweet brew.

Oh heavens.

The magical brew spread out through my body, and my worries of the moment receded to a comfortable distance. A rich royal purple aura surrounded Greg, and haloes of all colors glowed around the forms of everyone in the crowd.

I drank another mouthful of the heavenly gruit, fell to one knee, and said, "Greg Heath, will you marry me?"

He grinned and offered me a hand to help me up. "Don't spill that. Naw, Annabelle'd have my head. Get on to your date, girl."

"It is SO not a date," I said.

"Scoot."

I had to finish my cup before leaving the outdoor beer garden, then it was only another couple of blocks to the brewpub itself. Another crowd milled about the entrance, some folks sitting on the pavement, backs resting on the limestone façade.

Damn, Big Con hasn't even started, and I'm starting to get sick of crowds already.

I struggled my way to the host station and asked after Ernie. I was escorted by an adorable hostess in an elf costume to a booth in the back.

Ernie, the Night Duke of the Indianapolis vampire court, sat in the booth, wearing his cheap vampire suit costume and a top hat upon his head. Two zombies sat with him, both young women with torn street clothing and grisly makeup. The hat and the zombie-costumed gamers were surrounded by an unnatural black light aura that made me stop short of the table.

The Night Duke grinned and motioned for me to sit.

Chapter Three

My head spun; the floor was like the deck of a ship in a sudden tidal swell. Ernie watched me, eyes flicking to the seat. *Oh yeah, sit down, Skye, before you hit the floor. Heath's outdone himself with this brew.*

My butt plumped up the booth's seat cushion, causing the grisly sexed up zombie girl next to me to bounce up and down. Her eyes never focused on me, she just stared straight ahead at Ernie. The zombie girl across from me had only stoned eyes, looking past me, rather than at me.

"Ernie," I said, unnerved to find the Night Duke staring at me, eyes focused lower than my chin. I snapped my fingers in front of my boobs and pointed up. His eyes slid up to meet mine, then flicked away to scan the room.

"Good to see you again, Skye."

"Gonna introduce me?"

He smiled and met my eyes for another brief moment and chuckled.

Did that weasel just wink *at me?*

"Oh, Skye, this is Raven and Donna. They're my zombie guards."

I snorted. "I heard about the zombie rules supplement, but I didn't think anybody'd actually want to play one. Not much room for advancement, is there?"

Ernie lost his hauteur for a minute and became gamer-Ernie. I had the notion that if he had glasses, he would have pushed them up just then. "I don't think you read it very closely. Sure, all the lower levels are just brawn and nothing else, but you can take levels of sentience and even carry it on different paths. If I was starting over, I'd zombie my way up to Lich Lord. Great way to start the game, you don't have to know all the political ins and outs, you know? Like your consort."

Annabelle played the live action vampire game with us, but I think only to spend time with me. It's nice that she humors me at least, and being my consort in-game has perks. Not to mention the perk of everyone knowing she's who I'm really with, despite my in-game marriage to Ernie as the Night Duke.

I glanced at the two. "You two don't have to stay in character for my benefit. In fact, if Ernie said you had to, he's feeding you a line of—"

"Skye. They know the rules. I'm not toying with them—"

"Ha! That's BS and you know it! You toy with everyone!"

Ernie grinned. "Yes, I do. But it's more fun if you follow rules. These two, they're just very into their roles. Aren't you, girls?"

In unison, the zombie chicks raised their chins up once then dropped them.

I shivered, and not just because of the August sweat drying on my skin in Heath's air-conditioning.

"Look," I said, "You asked to meet me to tell me about Stuart. Spill it, Ichabod, or I'm out of the game for Big Con. I know you need me."

His lips pursed at the nickname. It fit his tall, lanky, gawky look, and I used it because I knew it stung. I'd feel bad about it later. Maybe. Right now, I was sick of being toyed with.

"Don't make threats, Skye, it's not pretty."

"I don't care about pretty. I'm awesome, even when I'm ugly. Tell me." I leaned forward in my booth and fixed him with what I hoped was an intimidating stare.

Just then, a miniature woman leaped onto the table, maybe a foot and a half tall. Minnie, my alter ego, the bit of me who lives full time in the fairy realm. I only get a glimpse when I've had a drink or three. When I can see her directly, I know I'm seeing a bit of the other world. Seeing auras from Heath's special brew clued me of course, but it being special, it takes less.

Minnie held a finger to her lips. I lowered my chin by a fraction of an inch and took my eyes off her. I paid attention in my peripheral vision, though, and she waved her arms over her head in a warning, doing a sort of pee pee dance.

What does she want?

Minnie pointed away from the table, off to the bar.

I glanced that way, caught her eye and shook my head once side to side. I'd already had a good enough drink.

Ernie snapped his fingers and I looked up at him.

"Something the matter, Skye?"

I shook my head. "No, just waiting for you to talk. I don't have to hang around here, I can just go, you know."

"Whatever."

I wanted to knock that top hat right off his head.

So I did.

"Don't be a bitch, Ernie. I'll walk." I rose from my seat.

Both girls' heads whipped around to look *right* at me, eyes focused for the first time since I'd gotten there.

Ernie grabbed at his hat and jammed it back on his head, eyes smoldering with quick anger. "Stop."

The zombie girl next to me reached out a hand and grabbed my wrist. Hard.

I looked over at her and she still just stared ahead, gaze somewhere past my shoulder and on into infinity.

"Hey, let go!"

Minnie's pee pee dance became an all out spazfest. She pointed with both hands past the bar to the restrooms.

Oh!

I yanked my hand away from zombie girl #1. Raven or Donna, I didn't know the difference.

At least I tried to. Her hand seemed welded to my wrist, and she held firm. My butt planted back on the cushion in the booth, hip to hip with her. I elbowed her, but she didn't budge. My head swam, my heartbeat pounded in my ears, and everything was doubled as my eyes lost focus.

I felt tiny Minnie hands on my other arm. From far away, it seemed, I heard her calling my name. My vision washed out in a haze, like I saw through some kind of sky blue field of energy. The skin contact between my wrist and the girl's hand grew warm, then hot.

Both girls and Ernie all gasped at the same time.

"Release her, Raven," said Ernie. The greasy smile on his face made my skin crawl. "What a shame."

Her hand unlocked and I leaped from the seat. I had to grip the table as the room washed up and down around me. The table was my anchor in choppy waters.

"I... I have to go powder my nose," I said.

Ernie rolled his eyes. "Look, it's like I said, these two are just way into their characters."

"Right. I'll be back."

He said something as I followed Minnie through the crowd to the ladies' room, but I didn't care to hear what it was. I rubbed my wrist only after the door shut behind us. Minnie hopped up on the counter, dodging a couple of puddles on the surface.

"Mins, he was about to spill."

"You've got to get away from him, biggun. He's not just playing the game; he's got some kind of mojo about him."

"I noticed his aura—"

"Bad mojo, hon. Big bad."

"But that's what Rebecca's got me looking for!" I said. *The mission is afoot!*

"Rebecca Burton? I should have known she'd be involved somehow."

I shook my head. "It's not like that, Mins. She says she felt a disturbance in the Force, and that makes me her padawan on the ground, poking around, reporting in. If it's just Ernie, I can handle him."

Minnie did something unbearably cute; she stomped her little foot on the counter. The expression on her face warned me not to laugh. "He's not just Ernie. He's Ernie with a loaded gun, waving it around like a toy. It's Ernie using power he doesn't understand."

The bathroom door slammed open. Raven and Donna stood shoulder to shoulder in the doorway. *Now* they looked right at me. They zombie-shuffled toward me, separating to come at me from two directions. Their mouths hung open, their arms outstretched to block me from getting past them.

I looked at Minnie, who knitted her fingers together, arms downward, like someone about to boost a friend over a wall.

Oh!

I mimicked her motion, and Minnie leaped into the air and bounded off my hands, straight at Donna. Or Raven, maybe.

The girl gave no reaction. No reaction that is, until Minnie sunk her tiny vampire fangs into the shoulder that lay exposed by her torn t-shirt.

I noticed a few things at once. One odd thing about the girls, other than dressing and acting like zombies, was that they had no aura at all. At the moment Minnie bit zombie girl #1, a black aura flared up as a spiral wreath of inky shadow obscured both of them. I also noticed the girl's eyes. Her icy blank stare melted to a fearful expression, her eyes fixed on me for a moment, then she swatted at the pinpricks of blood on her shoulder. She cursed a nasty blue streak, but I sighed in relief, though I couldn't have told you why.

If her friend cared, she showed no sign; she just kept shuffling toward me, arms outstretched.

Oh my God, is she drooling out of the corner of her mouth?

I'm no martial artist, but Rebecca taught me a thing or two during the "bootcamp" she put me through. I drew in a breath, became aware of my center of mass, and planted one gilded sandal into the zombie's diaphragm. She folded in the middle, the wind knocked out of her. Still, her arms flailed around and her gore-painted nails raked my calf, trying to grab me.

The ladies' room door banged open and swung shut. I heard shrill shouting out in the bar area.

Good. Maybe someone will come in here and scrape this crazy bitch off me!

Her breath came in ragged gasps while she fought to get her wind back, but the girl kept after me. My butt pushed into a cold, flat surface that gave a little behind me. A stall door. I pushed back fast and slammed the door in the zombie's face. She clawed and scrabbled at the dark stained wood of the door, and I fumbled for the lock. She shoved, and I shoved back. I had to get the bolt to line up with the latch, but she wasn't making it easy. In fact, for someone gasping for air, she was pretty strong.

Maybe too strong. The wood of the door groaned and I heard it crack with the strain.

I braced my feet on the toilet pedestal and threw my weight into it, and the door shut. Ready for this, I slid the bolt closed. I stayed braced against the door. The pressure from the other side stopped, and the wood groaned in relief.

SLAM!

My head whacked against the wood, and my eyes crossed for a moment. The crazy woman had thrown herself against the door.

SLAM! CRACK!

The screws of the hinges now showed give, and my right ear rang with the blow.

"Hey! Cut that out!" Heath's voice boomed from the bathroom doorway. I could have kissed him if I wasn't barricaded in a stall, hiding from a cosplaying lunatic.

I cried out to him. "Heath! She's crazy! Watch yourself!"

"Gotcha. Cops are on the way."

Cops? Wow this social call turned out to be a bad idea.

SLAM! CRACK!

A hinge screw fell to the floor with a silvery tinkle.

Another voice came from outside the bathroom.

Ernie whined, "Stop, Raven, stop it at once!"

I heard the girl take in a breath and shuffle away from the door. I dared a peek over the top.

Heath glared at Raven from the doorway, a wooden brewing oar in one hand, the other held the door open. Behind him, Ernie looked on with wide eyes, his top hat askew on his head. Raven slouched her way toward the two men.

A third man appeared behind Ernie. A football player, or at least someone cosplaying as one, wearing a blue jersey with white lettering, loomed behind lanky Ernie like a living wall of muscle. I had the strangest impression that his features had actually been chiseled from marble. His aura made me think of moonlight. A meaty hand flicked the top hat from the Night Duke's head.

Ernie's aura flickered to a more normal purple, losing the blacklight quality. Raven's aura ignited a brilliant canary yellow and she stopped in her tracks, drawing a breath. She stood up straight and began to cry.

"What's happening?" she groaned, "My shoulder hurts so much! I... oh my arm. I think it might be dislocated!"

Heath stared at her a long moment, then moved aside to let her out of the bathroom.

Ernie whirled to face the man mountain and stared him right in the 12 on his vast chest.

The big guy's voice probably registered on the Richter scale somewhere. "Got somethin' to say, ya twerp? You gamers make me sick, taking over downtown. And your stupid costumes. Get out of my way, I gotta pee."

"W-wrong bathroom, jerkwad," said the Night Duke.

Sporto's fist smacked into Ernie's head; The Night Duke collapsed to the floor like the end of a Jenga game.

"Hey, man, no fighting in my pub," said Heath, raising the oar to menace the big guy.

The big guy growled. I don't mean he made a grumbly noise in his chest. I mean he *growled like a bear.* I'll give Heath credit; he stood his ground and met the much bigger man's stare. Both men's auras flared.

I let myself out of the stall and stood behind Heath. I drew my fake sword and mimed Heath's oar-wielding stance. "Best not mess with the owner of the pub, dude," I said. "Do you really want to be banned and never drink another Heath brew?"

The massive football player wannabe blinked and looked at me, then back at Heath. "Oh. *You're* Heath? Hey, man, I didn't know. Hope we're cool, bro?"

Heath favored me with the ghost of a smile before looking back at the big guy, lowering his oar. "Yeah, we're cool. Just no fighting here. Take it outside."

The guy nodded, then both men looked down at the heap that was Ernie.

The Night Duke groaned.

Heath glanced at me. "Friend of yours?"

"I wouldn't go that far."

"Seen him around you," drawled Heath.

"Yeah, we're both in that vampire game."

Heath shook his head. "Bunch of trouble, if you ask me, but hey, what do I know?"

I glomped onto him to give him a surprise hug. "Heath knows Heath brews."

He shrugged me off, turning just a little pink in the ears. "Knock it off. You're lucky I like you, Skye. 'Cause I know you're trouble. I don't need trouble."

I smiled and shrugged. "Trouble is my business?"

"Still gotta pee," said the big guy.

Heath made a shooing motion. "I'm not cleaning it up. Go."

The man-moose fixed me with a strange look before stepping over Ernie. He reached down quick to grab at the top hat, but Heath stopped him with a hand on his elbow. "He's a jerk, but that's not yours, bud."

Ever see a bear look sheepish? Me either, at least not until right then. He nodded and thudded off toward the other bathroom.

Heath picked up the hat and toyed with it. "Guess I'll call off the cops after all. Can you take care of this guy? Gamer friend or no, he starts anything else, Skye, he's banned. His living dead girl groupies too."

I shrugged. "Like I care. Might be nice to have a place to go where he's not allowed."

Heath's faint smile warmed. "I'll keep it in mind. Listen, Skye."

"Hmm?"

"I'm not stupid. I know there's something more going on here. Be careful. Go see that Bask character."

"Bask? The Transit King?" *Crap, now he's going to think I'm crazy.*

"Yeah, him. Good guy, got a solid head on his shoulders, underneath that nutty act."

If you only knew...

I spied Minnie doing the Charleston along the bar behind Heath, trying to catch my eye.

"You know, I think that's the best idea I've heard all day. Except for one I just had."

"Yeah?"

"Could I have another Heather Gruit for the road?"

Heath mimed a toast with an invisible beer mug. "Sure. On the house, Skye."

Chapter Four

I sipped my big mug of heavenly heather infused honey beer and watched as the zombie girls got under Ernie's shoulders and helped him out of the room. Raven winced and glared my way.

"Since when do you bite people?" I asked Minnie.

She held out a shotglass, holding it with both hands. I tipped my mug and filled it with an ounce of frothy aromatic heaven. She took a long gulp of the stuff and belched before answering me. "Since you were about to become zombie meat, biggun."

"No, I mean—"

"Hey, you gotta use whatever weapons you've got when you're just three apples high! I inherited your pretend vampireness, so why not use my fangs if I gotta?"

"Well for starters, it kinda gives me the willies," I said.

A shadow blocked the light behind me, and I felt a large presence. "Know what gives me the willies? People who talk to themselves, am I right?"

A meaty hand grabbed my shoulder, and before I could react, I was spun around to face—

"Uncle Gonzo!" I cried, throwing myself on him, arms and legs wrapping around him. I pretended to gnaw on his shoulder, then thought of Minnie and stopped that.

Gonzo's not my uncle, or anyone's as far as I know, but in a way, he's *everyone's* uncle.

"Holy shit, Skye, did you go and get possessed *again*?" he said, thumping me on the back in his version of a hug. I clung onto him anyway. Over his shoulder, I saw another friend. A sad-faced red-headed pleasingly plump girl stood behind Gonzo. She produced a smile for me and did a little wave.

"Frannie! Aaaaaaa!"

"Jesus, Skye, now I'm going deaf," said Gonzo, shoving at me to get me to let go. "Augh, damned demon-addled girl, let *go*!"

I gave him one last squeeze and hopped off him to land on my feet, only to launch myself at Frannie, who put both hands up in front of her and cowered. She made a pitiful squeak, so I just gave her a quick hug and a laugh. I felt a familiar cobwebby tickling as I embraced her.

Both of my friends' auras crackled merrily, forest green on him, sunset orange on her.

Frannie's aura had that double-layered effect going on. Gonzo wasn't kidding about demonic possession. Both Frannie and I had been a demon's meat puppet. Frannie much more intensely than me. Once she'd gotten free, the demon had left a hole that her soul had leaked out over many months, leaving her mostly a shell, well on her way to becoming a ghoul. A Wiccan friend had patched the hole, but so much damage had been done that most of Frannie's soul lived *outside* her body as a ghost, guiding and speaking through her earthly vessel. She'd gotten the hang of it, and most people couldn't tell.

I'm not most people. Frannie and I have a kinship through surviving that supernatural ordeal. Minnie is the bit of me that leaked out after my possession. I still can't think about that night. I'm lucky because that night I was three or four sheets to the wind when it happened, so the memory is hazy and distant. But that's why I need to drink to communicate with Minnie or see into that other world.

And that's a funny thing no one's explained to me. Why's Frannie got a ghost, when I've got essentially a little fairy me as a companion? Why does Frannie see dead people while I see dark fairies and their world?

Gonzo jokes about ghosts and demons and possession because he doesn't want to believe in them. He knows on some level that they're real, but if pressed, he makes up excuses and does the verbal equivalent of sticking his fingers in his ears and going "La la la la!" But belief or not, Gonzo is someone I'd trust my life to, any day of the week. My biker knight in leather armor.

"You better watch out, Uncle Gonzo," I said, looking around as if I didn't want to be overheard. I put my fingers over my mouth and stage whispered to him, "There are strange things going on here."

Gonzo snorted. "What is it this time? Tinker Bell massing a fairy army to descend on Taco Bell so they can gas us all in our sleep?"

I laughed so hard that I couldn't finish talking right away. "Oh my God," I gasped out.

Even Frannie laughed, and her aura brightened as she did. "Geez, Gonz, you had to go there already?"

Gonzo shrugged. "What can I say, I'm always vigilant. Those little suckers will get you if you're not careful. Best defense is a good offense. Beer farts, anyone? Anything good on tap, Highlander?"

Gonzo can't resist nicknames, and my surname amuses him to no end.

"I, Skye MacLeod, says there can be only one," I said, between giggles. I pointed at the Heather Honey Gruit tap handle at the bar. Despite my heritage, I can't do a Scottish brogue to save my life. "'Tis the stuff of life, and it is your destiny to drink with me."

Behind the bar, Heath caught the hint, filling one mug, then another with his magical brew.

"Don't mind if I do," said Gonzo, settling in on the barstool next to mine. Frannie sat on my other side, which was around the corner of the end of the bar, so we could all see each other as we talked. Minnie folded her arms and sulked.

"Now what strange things are afoot at the Circle K this time, MacLeod?" he said, eyes on the filling beer mug, rather than me.

I felt just a touch insulted, because I don't dress this sexy every day. I decided to call attention to this fact. "You may have noticed my outlandish garb?"

He glanced at me and shrugged. "Is it phony vampire stuff again? 'Cause that's what I figured."

"No, dummy, it's for Big Con!"

I lost Gonzo completely for a long moment as Heath slid the first mug in front of him and he took a long, ecstatic drink of the beer. "Oh," he said, "oh God, this is ambrosia. Where have you been all my life?"

I should have talked to him before *introducing him to Heath's brew.*

"Skye to Gonzo, come in Gonzo, do you read me? Over."

He sat with his eyes closed and a beatific smile on his face for several beats then leaned over and planted a cold, beery smooch on my cheek. I caught Minnie's eye and she interrupted her sulk long enough to make exaggerated kissy faces at me.

Frannie laughed and said, "Congrats, Skye, you're Uncle Gonzo's favorite person today."

I smiled. "Glad you like it. So. Big Con."

He nodded and looked at me as though I'd just arrived. "Yeah, so? You know I'm not into all that make believe stuff. I'm here for the Grand Prix. Or more specifically, to show off my Norton at the biker bash on Meridian Street."

Heath slid Frannie her beer and wandered off to help other patrons.

"I came up for Big Con," said Frannie, "We're commuting the hour drive from Bloomington together, since there's no way we could get a room. All booked up, and even if there were, they're gouging out there."

"Hey, you guys could stay with me! Fantasy Freeform is paying for my room as part of my booth babe gig."

"Sweet!" said Frannie. "That explains the extra slut factor."

"Hey now! It's not slutty, it's *fantasy*!"

"If I weren't a gentleman, I'd make a joke about fantasies here," said Gonzo, between sips of gruit.

Frannie and I both laughed out loud.

"What? I'm a gentleman!"

I patted his stubbly cheek. "Gonzo, you're sweet, but you're so not a gentleman."

"I'm gentleman enough to take you up on your hotel room offer, and gentleman enough to not fart on your bed. Probably gentleman enough not to post pictures of you and Frannie spooning in the other bed."

"Who says there are two beds?" I winked at him.

Frannie giggled and fluttered her eyelashes at Gonzo.

Now Gonzo reddened. "Uh fine with me? But your girlfriend might kick my ass. Maybe Frannie's too, now that I think about it."

I laughed. "Annabelle isn't the jealous type. But she knows Fran's straight as a laser, and stuck on Jimbo. Speaking of your ubergamer boyfriend, why's he not here, Frannie?"

Frannie pouted. "His sister chose *this* weekend to get married, of all the weekends in the year. Jimbo almost boycotted the wedding on principle, but her fiancé asked him to be the best man. He looks delicious in his tux, but he's whined about missing Big Con every day for a month. I offered to go with him, but he said 'one of us ought to have fun' and so here I am."

I patted her shoulder. "That sucks! It's going to be huge this year. I intend to have a blast. That is, if my dear husband doesn't screw it all up for me."

"Husband?" Gonzo and Frannie said in unison.

I giggled. "Sorry. Vampire thing. We're married in game, it's a consolidation of power, gets me rank and influence, and it gets him bragging rights and cheap thrills."

Gonzo's eyes narrowed. "So, how far does the game require you to take that?"

I waved a hand in the air as if to erase the very idea as I took another sip of my beer. "Nah, Uncle Gonzo, it's not like that. He doesn't get to so much as hold my hand without me saying it's okay. Name only, in game. But he's acting weird, and seems to have some kind of mojo. That's what Minnie called it anyway. I think it's some kind of mind control. He had two zombie girls doing his bidding. One grabbed me and I felt weird for a minute. Then the two of them had me cornered in the ladies' room. One tried to bust down my stall door before Heath and some random sportsball goon intervened."

Minnie ended the silent treatment. "Hey! Don't forget about a feisty little biter. Augh, she tasted nasty. Speaking of, can I get a refill?"

"Sorry, hang on," I said, pouring another ounce of my dwindling gruit into her shot glass.

Frannie and Gonzo looked at each other. Frannie said, "Must be her fairy friend."

Gonzo squinted at the shot glass. "I see nothing."

Minnie raised the shot glass and shouted, "Cheers!"

Gonzo blinked and rubbed his eyes. "What the hell? That shot glass moved on its own!"

"It's Minnie. She's making a toast."

He drew in a breath and let it out. "Fine, okay. I can handle that. To friends and love," he said, raising his own glass. He clinked my raised mug and Frannie's, hesitated, then lightly tapped Minnie's shot glass.

Minnie grinned and let out a squeal of delight, then drank out of the glass.

After a long awkward moment as we all stared at Minnie's shot glass, Frannie asked, "So what was it about then? The grabbing and the bathroom attack?"

I shook my head. "I'm not sure, but he got me to meet him here by telling me he'd heard from Stuart's ghost."

Frannie sat up very straight. "Stuart? I guess I'd better keep a lookout."

I nodded to Frannie. "If you don't mind, hon?"

Minnie burped and said, "If he wasn't just BSing you. I think he wanted another zombie girl following him around, Skye."

"Who?" I said.

Minnie rolled her eyes. "You really are dense, biggun. He wanted to own *you*, dummy. He's always had the creepy hots for you, and it'd be nerd Christmas for him if he had his very own Skye to order around."

"What's she saying?" asked Frannie.

"Shhh. Hang on."

"This is such a load of crap. Talk to your imaginary friend later, okay Skye?"

Minnie shot Gonzo a nasty look, and I held up a finger to him. Guess which one.

"Minnie, that's scary. Is that what that blue glow was? A zombification spell?"

She shook her head. "No, that was your own aura, dear. I helped boost your resistance. That run in with the goose people taught me a thing or two about myself. I've got my own mojo."

"And if you hadn't helped out?"

She shrugged. "Dunno, but my guess is you'd be shuffling along behind the Night Duke, staring straight ahead. Or shuffling in front of him so he could watch, more like."

I shivered.

Frannie and Gonzo drank in silence, watching me talk to the shot glass.

"Guys, it's bad stuff. Ernie, my vampire hubby, has some kind of magic to enslave people, and he tried to use it on me. He's up to something, and I think it could get ugly fast."

Gonzo's voice came out in a whine. "Aw, do I have to get mixed up in a tipsy fairy tale?"

Frannie reached across the bar to touch his arm. "Don't be that way. You know better. This is real, even if you can't see it; it's a danger, even if it seems like pure fantasy. It's not a game, Gonzo."

Gonzo looked from her to me and said, "Look. I'm not going to leave you hanging, no matter how stupid it all sounds. But I'm out of my element. Just let me know what I can do. But how do I fight what I can't see?" he motioned toward Minnie and her half-empty shot glass.

"Just back me up, okay big guy?"

He nodded.

I held out my hand, palm up. Frannie moved her hand from Gonzo's arm to rest on top of my hand. Gonzo put his on top of hers. Minnie stood up and joined in.

"Okay, it's time for a bus ride," I said.

"You mean?" asked Frannie.

I nodded. "Got a date with a fairy king."

Chapter Five

After another round, I thanked Heath and we left his pub. I led Frannie and Gonzo to my hotel, got them keys at the front desk, and took them upstairs to show them the room, up on the fifteenth floor. I parted the curtains to reveal the skyline of Indy in all its glory. I could see the tiny forms of hundreds of gamers as they roamed her streets. All the lampposts I could see had been adorned by "Welcome Big Con!" banners.

"Ta da! We be stylin', my friends!" I did a flourish that would have made Vanna White proud, then flounced onto one of the beds.

Gonzo approved. "Not bad, Highlander, not bad!"

Frannie peered around in the corners, opened the closet door and shut it, and inspected each and every drawer in the room.

My eyes followed her nervous movements around the room. "What are you looking for? Fleas?"

Frannie stared at me, then shook her head. "Maybe I watch too much Supernatural, but I'm looking for objects that could have a curse on them. If Ernie's got mojo like that, we can't be too careful."

Gonzo laughed.

"I'm serious, Gonz."

"I know! That's what's so funny!"

Frannie stomped. "You said you'd help out!"

Gonzo sat on the other bed and stretched until it seemed like every joint in his body popped and snapped. He let out a happy sigh and said, "You know I will. Saved your ass a time or two. And I don't even *like* you."

"What? You don't like me? But Gonzo!"

"I'm shittin' you, sister. Granted, I thought Jimbo shoulda ditched you early on, but hey, everyone has an exorcist moment now and again. Chill out, you're fine. I got your back. Both of you."

During this exchange, Minnie had propped herself up on a pillow and had lip-synched along with the argument, her face contorting into comical parodies of my friends'.

I burst out laughing at her.

My friends glared at me.

"S-sorry! Minnie's being a goofball. I really wish you guys could see her, she's so funny!"

Frannie crossed her arms. "Well, *I* didn't find anything cursed in the room, but as Minnie reminds us, there could be invisible dangers."

I shrugged. "If there are, we'll handle them as they happen. I had a gargoyle in my hotel room last summer and I took him on wearing only a towel."

Gonzo winked at me. "I'd love to have seen that!"

Frannie smacked his arm. "Dirty old man!"

"Old? Old?" Gonzo feigned a chest wound.

"You heard me. You're almost old enough to be Skye's daddy."

I sidled up to Gonzo and batted my eyes. "Should I call you… daddy?"

Gonzo stood up and coughed, pacing the room. "No. Stop right there."

Frannie and I laughed.

"So, uh, what's next, girls?" Gonzo peered out the window.

"So, I've got to go see Bask. He's this little gnome guy, some people call him the Transit King."

Frannie said, "Do you just ride any bus and what, call out his name?"

I shrugged. "You know, I hadn't thought about it. I just sort of get on a bus and if I need him, there he is, sitting next to me. Well, and then there was the time he showed up on a gondola on the canal…"

"I ask," said Gonzo, "because my Norton Commander isn't going to polish itself for the bike show. If you're not about to rush into battle, I'll go do my own thing, and you can get a hold of me later."

"Yeah, that's fine, Gonz. I don't even know what we're up against yet."

"Want some company? I'd love to meet the Transit King," said Frannie, bouncing up and down a bit where she stood.

"Sure! Of course! The more the merrier. But I gotta admit I'm not sure what you'll see; it might just be like it is with Minnie here."

Minnie said, "But Annabelle talked to Bask before the battle with Queenie, she saw and heard him then. I bet she can meet him just fine."

I relayed what Minnie said to Frannie, then said, "I'd better pack a flask of vodka in case my buzz wears off. Oh, and once I leave downtown, I won't have the reality altering field of Big Con to protect me from the muggles, so I'd better change clothes."

Gonzo stared at me. "Reality altering—"

I laughed. "Just being cute. People are used to costumes during the con, downtown. Elsewhere, I'd draw way too much attention. Now why don't you shoo so I can change?"

Gonzo shrugged. "You know how to find me if there's trouble." He opened the door waved at us, then slipped out.

"Want me to give you some privacy?" asked Frannie.

"Just turn your back. I know it shouldn't really matter to her, but Annabelle's already annoyed with me, I don't need her getting the wrong idea, even if you're Straighty McStraighterson."

Frannie wrinkled her nose and stuck out her tongue at me, but turned around as I rummaged through the drawers. I changed from the FFF fantasy outfit into a pair of skinny jeans, some black Converse sneakers, and a blue TARDIS tank top. Annabelle teases me about the tiny placard on the Doctor Who police box's door that says, "Free for public use", and *everyone* asks me if I'm bigger on the inside. I've slapped more than one creepy nerd for using that line on me. But I know I look good in it, so screw all that. I gotta fly my geek flag during Big Con, you know?

I strapped on a special accessory, a belt with a holster that contained the Fairy Hilt. It's a scepter-like hand grip that works a bit like a light saber - but only to fairy folk. To anyone else, it seems like just a toy. I'd only ever used it once, to defeat the Queen of the Hunt, who'd enslaved my boyfriend Stuart. The Hilt came at a great price, as Stuart had sacrificed his life to give it to me in a last desperate moment.

Going to see my friend Bask, the Transit King, you wouldn't think I'd need it. But I haven't mentioned yet that Queenie was his wife, and he sicced me on her since he couldn't move on her directly. Call me paranoid, but better to be prepared for anything. I guess Rebecca's rubbing off on me.

Frannie nodded approval of my outfit, and Minnie hopped into my purse for the ride. We left the room and took the elevator down to the lobby. Turned out there was a special airport shuttle running for Big Con attendees staying at the hotels out there.

I decided that magic worked best if you didn't question it, and Bask had said I could find him on any public transit anytime I needed him. So why not?

We boarded the double-sized bus and found it almost empty. People were coming into Indy by the thousands, but not many were on their way outbound. I guessed that the few gamers on board were those who'd only come into the city to pick up tickets and badges on the day before the con, and now headed back to their airport hotel rooms. I got the thumbs-up from one guy, who said he liked my TARDIS tank top. I smiled, but found more isolated seats for Frannie, Minnie and me.

"So, do you have to be trashed for this to work?" asked Frannie, settling into her seat. She pulled out her iPhone, which was clothed in a metal tombstone case, and began poking at it.

"Nah, I think Bask would show himself to me, even if I was sober. He's not much to look at without booze, just a tiny homeless guy with an aluminum foil crown. Or is it shiny duct tape? Anyway, Heath's brew has me still seeing auras, so I should be good either way."

The bus started up after a few minutes. It pulled out of the hotel's breezeway still almost empty, which was fine with me. Easier to have crazy talk with a gnome with fewer people to overhear. I get tired of being the crazy person on the bus.

We rolled through downtown Indy, and the bus stopped a couple of times at other hotels to take on a couple of people here and there. Then we got moving, the bus being an express, it made no stops outside of downtown. I wondered if Bask would just appear next to me, or if he might get on at the airport itself.

"Well?"

I looked at Frannie. "Well, what?"

"Is he here? I don't see anyone like you described." Frannie poked at her phone without looking at me.

"No, not yet. I'm not sure what's going on."

"Maybe it's me. You could try moving to another seat?"

I hated to think bringing Frannie along would keep Bask away, but she had a point. "Yeah, okay."

I moved a couple of rows back, leaving an empty seat in case he needed a place to appear. From my experience, however, making a dramatic entrance wasn't a problem for the Transit King.

Time passed. We hit potholes here and there and the bus shook. Nothing happened.

I opened my purse and peered inside. "Mins, what do you think? Do I need to call his name? Wave my arms? Send up smoke signals?"

She showed me empty hands, palms up. "I got nothin', biggun. Maybe he's busy."

"What, like dedicating a new bus line?"

She laughed. "He's a fairy king. He's probably got lots of stuff to do, Skye. You were his priority because he needed you to do his dirty work."

"But, he helped me too! We're kin, kind of!"

"Sure, but remember that fairy part? Fairies are tricksy things. He's perfectly honorable, but to stay king, he's got to be perfectly focused on self-interest. Trust me, the minute you threaten his position, he'll sacrifice you like the pawn you are."

My heart sank. I liked to think of Bask as a friend. "Since when are you so cynical about fairies?"

Minnie shrugged. "Since I had my dealings with the goose people, I guess. Since I realized I'm not truly one of them. Since I've been thinking about that whole Queenie mess. Know who came out on top in that battle? It wasn't you, and it sure wasn't Stuart. And Queenie lost her head, leaving a big power vacuum."

The wheels turned in my head. "Bask. He got what he wanted, I guess."

Minnie touched her nose with a finger. "Bingo. And it cost him a magic token and some storytelling. And he has you as his sorta knight in the bargain."

I crossed my arms. "I hope you're wrong, Mins. I want to think the best of people. And Bask hasn't done anything to harm me."

Minnie nodded. "Let's hope it stays that way. I doubt he's got reason to go against you. I'd keep on his good side. Then again, you knocked off his wife, the Queen of the Hunt, so maybe he'd best stay on *your* good side, eh?"

I patted the Fairy Hilt at my side. "You know it, little bit." I sighed as the bus took an exit to go into the airport. "Just wish he'd show up soon."

The bus wound around the parking lots and ins and outs of the airport roads to pull up at the terminal. An electronic voice announced stops for passengers taking American, United, Lufthansa, making a short stop at each entrance. A few people got off the bus, but many more people got on at each stop.

Frannie turned in her seat, her eyes holding a question.

I shrugged and called, "Maybe on the way back?"

Just then, the electronic voice announced, "Passengers on Skye Air, please disembark now."

I checked the lit digital sign, and I saw that Skye was spelled right.

Frannie caught it too, and we both stood up, hanging on the overhead rail as the bus slowed to a stop. No one else stood. The doors opened, and even though I could see the airport out the windows of the bus, the rectangle of the doorway revealed a dark, torch-lit stone corridor.

Chapter Six

"So we just get off here?" said Frannie.

I grabbed her hand and pulled her toward the dark portal at a trot. "Yeah, follow me."

If the bus driver noticed, she gave no sign, eyes ahead, not even acknowledging the "thank you" I called to her.

I stepped down into the dark corridor, still dragging Frannie behind me by her hand.

She said, "You think he's at the airport… Oh my God, Skye! What happened? Where are we?"

I guess it worked. I turned around to face her and instead of the bus I only saw more corridor stretching off behind her.

"I'm not sure, but I'll bet King Bask is around here somewhere."

The place had a musty, damp smell about it, like a swampy basement, with fainter, older, harder to place scents mingling in. The flames from the torches gave off no odor I could detect.

Frannie's mouth hung open as she looked both ways down the hall. "This is like, some kind of dungeon?"

With that word, it came to me. This place looked exactly like the dungeons at Queenie's castle in Holliday Park. I'd been held in a disgusting cell for awhile before I escaped.

A flapping, slapping sound came from the direction I'd been facing when we stepped off the bus. I knew that sound, and an icicle of fear shot down my spine and into my feet. I drew the Fairy Hilt and a light blue blade of energy faded into view.

"What's that for? What's wrong, Skye?"

"Incoming. Get back, okay?" I said, putting myself between Frannie and the approaching footsteps from around the curve of the hallway.

A frogman, dressed in studded leather armor, came marching into view, his broad amphibian face lit with the flickering light of the torches on the walls. His bright steel-headed pole ax flashed orange as it caught the light. He seemed unfazed by my magic sword, but he did come to a halt about two sword-lengths away from me.

"The King will grant you audience," the frogman said in a burping sort of voice. "Follow me."

Froggy spun on his flat foot and marched back the way he came.

I sheathed the Fairy Hilt and the blue light it gave went away.

"Did… did you see that?" said Frannie.

"Yeah. What did it look like to you?"

"A frog in armor with an axe?"

"Okay, you see what I see while you're here. Good. Let's go."

We followed the flapping steps of the frogman guard around the bend, up a spiral staircase, and into a large chamber, its roof supported by a dozen columns. Light filtered in through high slitted windows, perhaps two stories above us. The frogman guard led us down a long green carpet strip to a layered dais, which reminded me of a cake. The cakelike dais was topped not with a bride and groom, but a massive throne of stone. Rich green velvet padding backed the seat, and lost in its vastness was a tiny figure I recognized.

"Well lassie, looks like ye came jest in time, and ye brought yerself a friend, didn't ye?" Bask's laugh boomed and echoed throughout the hall. No dwarfish beggar sat above us, but a regal gnome in purple robes with golden trim and shining gems for buttons. No longer seeming to be made of aluminum foil, the golden crown on his head sparkled in an unseen light. He stank of wealth and power.

"You're looking well, Bask. Nice digs. Did you get tired of riding the bus?"

A frogman stood by the King's side, holding a golden tray full of meats and cheeses, as well as several goblets and what looked like a bottle of wine. Bask took a goblet and shooed the guard away. The frogman plodded down the steps to our level and offered us goblets and food.

"Drink with me, Skye, we have much to discuss. Yer friend is someone special too, isn't she? Heh, she's got me seein' double, I'd say. Neat trick, I've got ta know what makes her tick."

I folded my arms. "This seems wrong. I thought we were friends, O Transit King."

King Bask set his goblet on the arm of his great throne with a clank. His smile faded, and the room seemed far darker than it had before, as though the sun had gone behind a cloud. A storm cloud, light flashing in his eyes. I thought of my conversation with Minnie on the bus. About how dangerous a friendly gnome might be in truth. About how his domain lay in transit and that we had gossiped about this powerful being in one of those places of power for him. Along a straight track, ruled by an elder creature. One likely beyond my comprehension. One who'd had his own wife killed, and now lived in her castle and bossed around her former guards. Guards with axes. I wished I hadn't put away the Fairy Hilt now.

Then Bask laughed. "Oh, that we are, Skye MacLeod. And kin ta boot. Yer one of my favorite mortals. Mostly mortal, ha! Knew you wouldn't put up with pomp an' circumstance." The sun came out from behind the clouds, the light in his eyes faded to a merry twinkle, and he hopped up out of the throne, leaving the fancy robes behind. He wore a green vest over simple brown breeches, his feet clad in sandals, a silly pointed cap upon his head. He could have been a leprechaun or a tiny Robin Hood. Bask snatched up his goblet, which sloshed but did not spill, and he took a great gulp of its contents before descending toward us.

Despite the look of great age about him, he danced down the steps of the dais with a youthful vigor. I had the image of a child in a Halloween costume, though his giggles were far too deep to be that. He stopped on the final step and looked up at me. "Yer a sight fer sore eyes, and no mistake, Miss Skye. Ye think it be easy sittin' here and directin' traffic about the city? Not ta mention, aeroplanes comin' and goin', trains pullin' in an' out. It's a bigger world, more like the old days in a way. Jest more and more and more, ya know? Makes lots fer a codger like me ta do. I've missed ye, lass, been meanin' to pay ye a visit."

Bask raised his goblet. "C'mon, less find somethin' a bit cozier, eh?"

He walked toward a side door, waving away a couple of Frogman guards. "I ken handle meself again' a couple of lovely lassies, ye ax-wieldin' amphibians. Go patrol er something, hey?"

The Frogmen backed off, but their shiny black eyes seemed laser focused on Frannie and me. Frannie slipped a sweaty hand in mine. I glanced at her, and saw that not only was she pale and shaking, but her aura had separated. A second sunset-colored outline of Frannie trailed a few paces behind us now.

Like a ghost. Well, exactly like a ghost. But I'm not supposed to be able to see into the Shadow realm, am I? Just the Fairy world, when I'm under the influence. Then again, Frannie and I have the same sort of demonic origin story, sisters forged by Shadows. Or maybe it's just Heath's brew that gives me that edge. I don't see auras without whatever's in the gruit, anyway.

Bask opened the side door, which led to another corridor that had steps up at intervals. It widened and through an arch, we came to a grand entry hall. One I recognized from my previous visit to Queenie, when she ruled this place. I thought of the cell deep underground where I'd been imprisoned. I might still be there today, alive or dead, if I hadn't had an unexpected ally on the inside. I thanked my lucky stars that I made friends so easily. I squeezed Frannie's plump hand in appreciation. She turned her head and managed a weak smile.

"Hang in there, Franster. Just trust me, it'll be all right. I promise."

She nodded and squeezed my hand once more, then let go, some color having returned to her face.

More guards pulled open massive wooden doors, and a shaft of bright sunlight flooded the room. Frannie and I squinted against it, but the Transit King trotted on out into the daylight. The August heat made the dank castle seem more inviting, but I felt safer outside.

Outside was Holliday Park. The late afternoon sun filtered through the trees, and the air was soup-thick with humidity. Behind us, I saw the faint outline of the castle superimposed on the fake ruins that served as a centerpiece for the neighborhood park. People picnicked on blankets in the grass, kids ran to chase Frisbees, and runners trotted past on the pavement nearby. Bask led us down a footpath worn in the grass, toward a picnic table in the shade of a willow tree. As we brushed past its leafy tendrils, sounds from outside became muffled and distant, the air less oppressive, and tension melted in my shoulders.

We sat at the table. Bask brushed away a few flakes of peeling paint and stray willow leaves and set down the tray of food and drink.

"Now will ye have a drink and a bite with yer ol' friend Bask?" His grin put me at ease.

Frannie said, "I'd be delighted. Pleased to meet you, your highness."

"That'd be 'yer Majesty,' if I were standin' on tradition. But jess call me Bask, or Transit King if ye please, while we're cozy like this, hey?" He offered her a goblet, and she raised it toward her lips.

I put a hand over the goblet to stop her from drinking. "Bask, I hate to be a pain, but fairy food and drink? I heard that was a bad idea for mortals like us."

Bask's laugh came from deep within his belly and his eyes crinkled with mirth. "I taught ye well, or mebbe yer little friend did. She ken come out of yer bag an' join us, ya know."

Minnie peeked out of my purse, looked up at me, then hopped out onto the table and sat cross-legged. Bask unscrewed the cap on the bottle of wine and poured a bit into it for Minnie, which she accepted with a smile.

Bask held up the bottle, which turned out to be a Trader Joe's brand of wine. "Got this stuff jess fer ye mortal folk, 'specially since I knew my Skye might be a wee bit leery of anythin' I might have. Cheese, ham and bread are from the Safeway on the IndyGo 28 line, if ye want ta know." His eyes, still twinkling met mine. "Scout's honor!"

I took my hand away and took the goblet he offered me. "Sorry to doubt you, Bask. Just seemed like you'd changed a bit back there in the throne room of your wife's old castle."

"Heh, ye have me there. And time fer a toast, I think." He raised his goblet and his voice, saying, "Here's ta Queen Howl, whose hunt came ta a bad end. She were a fine woman, but power went ta her head. I'da liked ta have saved her, but tsk, we can't save everybody, in the end."

We clinked metal goblets together, and made sure to tap Minnie's screw top cap, and drank all at the same time. The dry red wine burned as it filled my mouth and slid down my throat.

Nothing magical about this stuff. Two Buck Chuck is fit for a fairy king?

"Ahhh that's th' stuff!" cried Bask, wiping his mouth on his sleeve. He turned to peer at Frannie. "Now yer a mystery, aren't ye? Skye's manners be slippin', the ole Transit King is at a disadvantage."

Manners? Oh!

"Sorry! King Bask, meet Frannie. She's a friend I met a couple of years ago, in Chicago."

Frannie offered a hand to shake, but the little guy stood up on the picnic table's bench, took her hand in his, and kissed it. "At yer service, fair lady. Chicago, eh? That explains yer second self. Or mebbe yer first self?"

She blushed and murmured, "Pleased to meet you. And yeah, something like that."

The two of them locked eyes a long time. The silence became awkward, then uncomfortable. I started to worry about fairy magic again, but Frannie's expression betrayed no great distress, only curiosity and embarrassment. Bask smiled and plopped his butt back down on the bench and laughed. "I'd say there be advantages to yer sitch, Frannie me lass. Bein' two of yourself, ye kin watch yer own back, hmm? Better be watchin' Skye's back, 'cause she can't see where ye can see, d'ye follow?"

Frannie paused, still a bit in a daze, then nodded. "That's sort of why we're here."

The Transit King picked up some meat, possibly a Slim Jim, from his royal platter and nibbled on it. "Is it? Tell me more."

"It's Stuart," I began.

Bask turned and looked straight at me, meat snack forgotten. "Aye? Yer lost love?"

I nodded and took another gulp of the wine. "Ernie says he saw him, spoke with him. His ghost, that is."

"Now how's Ernie, yer phony baloney husband, got a line on the world o' ghosts an' shades?"

"I was hoping you might know. Something's different about him. Minnie says he's got some kind of mojo now; he had a couple of girls made up to be 'sexy zombies' at his beck and call. He said they were just role-playing as part of our game, but they tried to attack me in the bathroom until he called them off."

"Jealous, mebbe?"

I shook my head. "No, it was something else. Trying to grab me, capture me maybe."

Minnie said, "Tell him about the hat!"

"Oh yeah, he's affected a top hat, you know, like a cheesy movie vampire? Except when the hat's off his head, the girls change, their auras change, they lose their zombie intensity."

Bask, taking a drink from his goblet snorted. "Magic hat, eh? Where'd he get somethin' like that, off eBay?"

Frannie laughed.

"No clue. But I think I've underestimated the Night Duke. He's up to something, and I need to figure out what it is."

"If he's seein' Stuart an' zombifyin' gamer lasses fer fun, mebbe yer out o' yer depth, Skye me girl. Here, lemme offer ye help."

He reached into the neck of his tunic and came out with a rectangular silver pendant, hanging on a chain around his neck. He took this off and dangled it before him.

I leaned in to get a better look. It was a tiny silver flask. A bull's head was circled by a belt that bore the words, "Hold Fast".

He held it out further toward me. "Take it."

"The MacLeod family crest?" I said, reaching out to touch it. He laid the warm metal flask in the palm of my hand, and let go the light chain, which pooled around it. Though the little thing could hardly contain an ounce of liquid, it felt heavy in my hand.

"Aye, the flask is yer family's, Skye. But the liquid inside belongs to the fairy world, 'tis my own concoction. Very old, very rare, and very strong. The silver of th' flask, and the crest upon it may bring ye fortune and some help again' those from Shadow. Remember always the words, yer clan motto an' hold fast."

"Thank you, King Bask," I said, a little in awe of the artifact I held.

He held up a finger. "Dinna thank me yet. The brew is on loan, jess in case. An' ye drink it, ye owe me another favor, like before."

Minnie covered her mouth with her hands and shook her head. I remembered our talk on the bus, and I could just hear her warning me about deals with fairies.

"What's so special about it, then?"

"'Tis a sort of magical liquor. Call it th' wonderbooze. With yer special powers an' fairy heritage, Skye, ye should be able to fade into the fairy realm an' back. Ye'll be unstoppable fer a few minutes, I expect. 'Tis special to me, lass, but should you need it, use it. But then ye'll be in me debt again."

"Aren't you already in *my* debt for taking care of Queenie?"

Bask looked like I'd slapped him. Frannie drew in a sharp breath. Minnie wiggled her bottom to move further away from both Bask and me.

"Ye be kin, and ye be a frien', Skye, but there's no call fer that kind o' talk. I dinna ask ye to do that, it was what ye had ta do, it was what was right. This is fairy business, favor for favor. Ye can refuse, an' I'll have that flask filled wit' yer favorite vodka an' we'll have no favors standin' between us. Yer choice, lass."

I looked at Frannie, but her wide, frightened eyes held no answers. I turned to Minnie, who'd scooted nearly to the edge of the table, still clutching the wine bottle's cap. She shook her head to one side, then the other.

Wonderbooze? Well, at least I don't have to decide right now, I can just not drink it, and if all this blows over without me needing it, I can just keep the flask and return the booze later—Bask interrupted my thoughts with a clap of his hands. Frogmen approached. "Better tell me now, lass. 'Tis always a pleasure visitin' with ye an' yer little bit, an' 'twas a delight ta meet yer lovely friend an' her ghost, but th' roads must roll, an' I'm th' Transit King, y'know?"

He hopped down from the picnic table bench and dusted himself off. One of the Frogmen gathered the goblets, the tray, and even Minnie's bottle cap.

"I'll take it, and I'll try not to use it," I said.

Bask nodded, eyes meeting mine for a long moment. "Owin' yer kin a favor isn't the end of the world, is it, Skye?"

"Last time I owed you a favor, my boyfriend died," I said.

His mouth pressed into a hard line. "Hmm. An' ye think it was my doin'?"

"I think the stakes get high when favors get owed to fairy royalty. Even friendly fairies."

Bask held my eyes for several heartbeats and then nodded and chuckled without humor. "Yer learnin', lass. But between life or death, I advise ye ta pick usin' me favor to survive, hey?"

I nodded. "And I appreciate it."

He smiled and waved. "Fare well. An' ye need a ride, th' bus fare's on me. Oh an' Skye? Don't be too free with tha' Fairy Hilt. It works best if ye've got an army at yer back. The fair folk hate it; ye'll make no friends if ye flash it around. An' remember, ye've got to sleep sometime."

Before I could ask for explanation, Bask and his guards turned and walked back toward his ghostly castle and the more solid-looking fake ruins.

Chapter Seven

Despite objections from Minnie, we took Bask up on his offer and rode the #28 downtown. It felt like *déjà vu*, but at least this time I didn't stink of smoke or sewage. I asked Minnie about Bask's parting comments about the Fairy Hilt, but she had no idea. I asked her to look into it and she smiled and said, "My meat, boss, I'll see what I can dig up."

Along the way, my phone rang.

Annabelle.

I picked up. "Hey babe! How's the shift going?"

"It's quiet. Look, I'm sorry for being such a bitch earlier. You're trying, I know you are." Her voice made me feel warm inside, even if her words had the potential for another stressful conversation.

"It's okay. I've got a mission on top of the booth job."

"Rebecca? Holy crap. What's going on?"

"She has me on the lookout for boogeymen and things that go bump in the night. Think I found one already."

I heard her take in a breath. "Shit, Skye, what is it?"

"It's Ernie. He's up to something, and it's more than just being creepy."

"What, is Rebecca in on your gaming now?"

I laughed at the idea. "No, he's got some dark magic that's stirring up trouble, and I'm pretty sure that's what Rebecca's after."

"Well, more work is good, but her kind of work is dangerous."

"Says my girlfriend, the sexy firefighter."

"You know what I mean!" I heard the smile in her voice. I couldn't help smiling in response.

"I know. I will be careful. Check in with you later, sweetie."

We hung up just as the bus reached our stop downtown. I realized I hadn't had a bite to eat since morning. Frannie didn't want to go back to Heath's so soon, and I didn't want to hit the food court on the eve of Big Con, so we wandered around the area. I suggested sushi, but Frannie made a face and said, "No, nothing raw, please."

I'll admit I got a bit whiny about needing to eat, and now. Then Monty's pub came into view. It's a sort of cooperative competitor of Heath's, a big place that's a bit out of the way. The owners are friends, and though they both try to outdo each other to be *the* Big Con gathering spot, there's plenty of business to go around.

"The night before Big Con is the best time to get into Monty's," I told Frannie, "Not enough con-goers are in town yet. Tomorrow, this place will have an hour or two wait to be seated."

We arrived to find a culture clash in progress. Gamers both with and without costumes sat to one side of the patio seating area, and the other side was claimed by dozens of people, mostly guys, wearing blue and white football jerseys. Both sides eyed each other with suspicion and annoyance.

Star Trooper guards, dressed in their black plastic armor, seemed to hold the line between the two groups, looking fierce. They had no choice, the faces on their helmets was frozen in fierce scowls. As we walked up to the hostess station, one enormous Trooper stepped out in our path and held his laser rifle sideways to block us from going further.

"We don't serve your kind here," said the tinny voice of the Trooper.

I drew the Fairy Hilt, which failed to produce its blue glowing blade. A sure sign I'd lost my buzz. Still, I went with it. I fell into a sword-fighting stance. "My laser sword says otherwise," I said in my best basement-dwelling-nerd imitation.

The Trooper made some reply, but I missed what it was. Every single football fan on the patio stood up and looked right at me, mouths gaping open. For a moment, I thought I must still have my booth babe outfit on, but no. I glanced at my purse to ask Minnie, but she'd disappeared along swith the last effects of Heath's brews and the sip of cheap wine I'd had earlier.

Frannie and the Trooper turned to see the crowd of sports fans staring at me, too.

So, it's not just me.

The Star Trooper lowered his rifle, and I sheathed the Hilt.

The football fans murmured among themselves and went back to what they'd been doing.

The tinny voice said, "What the hell was that, Skye?"

I peered into the lenses of his mask and said, "Phil?"

"Huh? Oh yeah," he reached up and raised the mask of the science fiction armor to reveal Phil's smiling face. "That was freaky. Think they've never seen gamers before?"

I made a sweep of my arm to take in the dozens of gamers on the patio. "Uh, duh? I dunno, maybe they think your gun is real?"

"What makes you think it's not?"

"Phil, it's clearly a super soaker painted black."

"Good point."

Frannie frowned, her arms crossed.

"Oh! Frannie, this is Phil. He's my boss for the booth babe gig. Phil, this is Frannie, she's from Bloomington and sees dead people."

Frannie swatted my arm. "You don't have to tell *everyone*!"

"Phil's seen some strange things; he's one of the few who'll believe that."

Phil shrugged. "I won't say it's impossible."

Frannie smiled. "Join us for dinner?"

Phil shook his head. "I'd love to, but I'm on duty."

Frannie laughed. "Seriously."

"Monty's paying the Legion to show up here in force throughout Big Con, and we're giving the money to a children's literacy charity. I'm doing most of my volunteer shifts during dinnertime, since the dealer hall will be closed by then."

I said, "Makes sense. Skye hungry. Needs food badly."

Phil saluted us and the hostess showed us to a patio table. I caught some of the sporty-sports glancing my way every so often.

"Must be my killer Doctor Who tank top," I said to Frannie.

She shrugged. "It's kinda creepy. That guy over there won't look away, even when I catch him staring."

I scanned the crowd. I spied what seemed to be the same man-mountain in the 12 that'd socked Ernie at Heath's earlier, staring right at me. His face betrayed no emotion or interest in me personally. He just watched me. I stuck my tongue out at him. He blinked, but didn't look away.

"Creepy creepy," I said.

"Just ignore the muggles; they're probably not used to seeing geeks out in large numbers."

I nodded, but shifted to another seat with my back to that side of the patio.

Monty's is famous for their enormous gourmet cheeseburgers, and the ones we ate lived up to that reputation. Oh my mercy, when it arrived, I devoured my massive blackened blue cheese burger. I'd eaten half of it and a handful of fries before even taking a sip of the beer that came with it.

Frannie stared at me, only a couple of bites into her mushroom Swiss black bean burger.

"Wha?" I said around half a dozen fries I'd just stuffed in my mouth.

She shook her head and said nothing, but her eyes spoke volumes. I'd disturbed her.

I chewed, swallowed and washed the fries down with some excellent brown beer. "Come on, out with it. Did I grow horns or something?"

"It's just... it's just that you reminded me of a bad time. The hunger. You never got that far."

When Frannie had been one of a couple friends who'd been possessed by the same demon that made me its bitch a few years back, I'd been taken care of very soon after, and only had Minnie and my otherworldly senses as a result. The others slowly degraded into a sort of undead state, what they called a ghoul. Those on the road to ghouldom craved raw and preferably rotten meat. The hunger could be overpowering, and from Frannie's haunted look, it'd be polite if I slowed down.

"Aw, I'm sorry Frannie. I didn't think."

She forced a smile. "I know you didn't mean anything by it. Thought I'd be less sensitive by now. Post traumatic ghoul syndrome, I guess."

I reached to pat her hand, but Minnie appeared in between us. She pointed behind me, jumping up and down. "Skye, you dummy, turn around!"

A line of big guys in football jerseys advanced upon another line of costumed Star Troopers, toy rifles held in front of them in a symbolic barrier.

Except those weren't guys. Not human guys. Seven feet tall and more while hunched over, these stony monsters in blue jerseys loomed over the Star Troopers. Their black eyes held insect-like facets like gemstones, their tusks jutted above and below their lips. Trolls. No other word fit.

Only one troll resembled human size and shape, though I saw him change before my eyes, tusks growing out of that sculpted marble visage, eyes revealing facets.

I had drinks at Heath's, so why didn't I see him as a troll before?

The trolls shoved at the Star Troopers, who fell over backward, armor clattering and scraping on the pavement. They scrambled to stand, hindered by the bulky plastic costumes, but the trolls stepped past.

Toward me.

I put my hand on the Hilt and they stopped.

Behind me, Frannie's voice trembled. "Skye, why are those Colts fans coming at us?"

Marblehead stepped ahead of the ranks of the bigger trolls and said, "Will you break the chain?"

"Huh?" I said, feeling less than brilliant.

His voice boomed in the patio courtyard. Everyone I could see had turned to watch the spectacle. "You have the means, but will you do it? Or will it be war?"

"Dude. What are you talking about?"

"You cannot avoid choosing sides, mortal. Not if you wield ancient power. You will break the chain or we shall take the power from you by force."

Minnie climbed my arm and whispered in my ear. "Time to go, biggun. Discretion being the better part of valor. And staying alive."

My jaw clenched, my teeth gritted. An image of the flask around my neck came to my mind's eye. "Hold Fast" it said. My family motto. What would my ancestors do?

They'd hold fast!

My hand tightened on the Hilt. *Maybe I could take out Marblehead as an example…*

Minnie guessed my thoughts. "No, Skye! You're outnumbered, and any one of these guys could overpower you."

Frannie agreed. "Umm, Skye, I'm laying down some money for dinner. Let's get out of here."

I thought of Stuart, bleeding to death, stabbed by Queenie. I'd won against her, but my heroics cost his life, not mine. I wasn't ready to see Frannie or Minnie die for me over some football-loving troll's challenge. Not here. Not now.

Maybe "Hold Fast" meant to hold against aggression, but why wait for it to happen?

I grabbed Frannie's hand and dragged her off behind me. I called over my shoulder, "I'm not playing your game, rock-head! It's not my fight!"

None of the trolls followed, but Marblehead called after me, "When night falls tomorrow, you will be made to choose, scion of MacLeod!"

Now how did he know my name?

Frannie's short legs pumped to keep up with my longer ones, but that confrontation motivated us both.

We ran toward the city's center and hit Meridian, which was lined with motorcycles of all description, in both directions, as far as I could see. I dodged around Terminator lookalikes, tough girls in bright bandanas and tight jeans, guys with ZZ Top beards, and even a guy with a leather jacket and a ponytail.

"Gonzo!" I collided with my bearlike friend and hugged him tight for the second time that day.

"Hey hey, what the hell, Highlander? What's chasing you? The boogeyman?"

"Trolls," I said.

"Football goons," said Frannie.

Gonzo stared at us. "What? Are you drunk?"

I shook my head. "That's the problem, I got sober."

Gonzo laughed. "Skye, you're a girl after my own heart. Sobriety is a problem all right; it's ruining this great nation of ours. I say we have a drink and talk about it."

I slapped at his leather-clad shoulder. "This is real, Gonz!"

He scanned the crowd in the direction we'd run toward him. "I don't see trolls or football goons," he said. "What did you do now?"

"Nothing! I mean, we saw the Transit King, we ended up in Holliday Park, we bussed back downtown, we stopped at Monty's for a bite to eat, and these trolls just knocked over some Star Troopers and…"

Gonzo put his fingers over my mouth. "Skye. Breathe. You're making no sense. Come on."

I followed Gonzo and Frannie followed me. A few biker types stared at us as he pulled me into what looked to me like Celtic Hooters. We were seated at the bar by a girl in a tiny, daring little plaid skirt and tight, low-cut black top with a clover logo. And cleavage. Miles of cleavage.

All the waitresses wore the same outfit, and most of them had red hair, though I doubted many had been born that way.

I've got *to take Annabelle here sometime.*

Gonzo ordered and we each got set up with a shot of Irish whiskey. Not my usual poison, but after missing a bunch of trolls right in front of me, I thought a bit more fortification couldn't hurt.

Frannie whined. "But Gonzo, I don't drink whiskey."

"You'll drink your whiskey like a good girl or you'll hurt your Uncle Gonzo's feelings."

She pouted.

Minnie hopped on the bar and glanced at me. I nodded to her. She sipped at the whiskey and floated an inch or two off the bar.

I'd never seen her do that before.

We all clinked shot glasses and drank. Gonzo's disappeared like a magic trick. Frannie took several sips, and each sip made her scrunch her face and gasp for breath.

Mine went down in a long gulp, burning a trail across my tongue, igniting the back of my throat and smoldering in my gullet. I took in a breath to thank Gonzo, but the alcohol vapors made my head even lighter and I coughed.

Gonzo smacked the shot glass down and grinned at me. "Now. Tell me your story."

I laughed and told him each detail, one after another, rather than spilling it all out at once. He snorted and rolled his eyes at parts that he couldn't swallow, mostly involving the Transit King, but his brow furrowed and his eyes glinted with anger when I told how the trolls threatened me. "What's their damage? What chains are they talking about? Sounds like an easy choice to me."

"Choice? I was *there* and I don't know what choice they meant, Gonz!"

"Easy, Skye. They want you to do something. Whatever it is, they're threatening you to do it. Civilized folks don't do that. They ask for your help. I'd say the right choice is to do whatever these guys don't want you to do."

I turned my shot glass up to let the last drop of the Irish drip onto my tongue, thinking this over. "So how do I find out what they want me to do?"

Frannie surprised us both, by saying, "Find one and follow him."

Chapter Eight

After the sun set, Frannie, Gonzo and I stood in the shadows across the street from Monty's. Gonzo caught on quick that my power was fueled, or at least enabled, by alcohol, so we'd stopped off at a liquor store and got some whiskey. Not the expensive stuff we'd had at Celtic Hooters, but some Canadian rye whiskey he favored when on a budget. Frannie insisted on getting herself a Big Gulp at a convenience store, as a mixer, but Gonzo and I just drank straight from the bottle.

"This… This is a bad habit, Skye," said Gonzo, handing me the bottle.

I drank again and my vision swam. Not from visions of the fairy realm, but from too much too fast. *Keeping up with Uncle Gonzo might not be the best idea I ever had.*

Frannie just sipped at her spiked Big Gulp.

When I felt I could speak without a rasp, I said, "Yeah. Okay. I think I'm good. You know, I'm the only one who *has* to drink to do this."

Frannie shook her head. "You think I'm trailing after trolls, or even football goons, while I'm sober?"

"Yeah, and if you think you could talk me into believing half of this fairy tale without a buzz on, you're more delusional than I thought." Gonzo cackled.

Just for good measure, I put the bottle in my big purse before there could be another round.

"So where are they?" Frannie asked.

I thought a moment. "Gonz, you weren't here earlier, you could go ask one of the Star Troopers if they know anything."

"Yeah, okay, that works." Gonzo nodded and then snuck down half a block in the deepening gloom and crossed the street. As we watched, he talked with one of the sci-fi gamer guards. Both of them gestured and I saw the Trooper point off down the street.

Gonzo saluted and then made a beeline across the street, getting honked at by a passing car on his way, and said, "City

Market. The dork guard guy said after you left, the football guys headed toward City Market."

"Do you think they went to the catacombs?" said Frannie, slurring her speech more than I would have expected. Or maybe I'd had enough that I couldn't tell for sure.

"Catacombs? What catacombs?" I said.

"Oh, no!" said Minnie, still hanging out on my shoulder. She'd refused further alcohol after the whiskey in the bar, and had been quiet since then.

"What's wrong, Mins?"

"That's a bad place," she said.

Frannie said, "The catacombs are a remnant of early Indianapolis. Under City market, there is a vast storage space, with tunnels leading off as far as Union Station. Goods used to come in on trains and got carted underground to be sold at market later. Being cool down there, produce kept better too."

"So an underground railroad for food?" I said.

Frannie scowled at me. "If you knew your Indy history, you wouldn't joke about the Underground Railroad that way. It was a real thing that was real."

Gonzo snickered. "You just said…"

"I know what I said! But these catacombs are rumored to be haunted."

Minnie murmured in my ear, "Not haunted by the dead. It's an Unseelie haven."

"Unseelie?"

"What?" said Gonzo and Frannie at once.

"Uh, Minnie's talking to me, sorry."

Frannie said, "What's she say?"

"Says Unseelie types live there. Dark fairies. Well, darker than usual."

Gonzo said, "You mean, like trolls?"

Frannie and I stared at Gonzo.

"Yes!" said Minnie.

I relayed this.

"Well, why did we have to stake this place out if she knew?"

Minnie giggled. "You didn't ask, biggun!"

"She's being a smart ass," I said. "I think we should…"

A sudden chill went through me, despite the soup warm summer night.

Frannie gasped. "Uh, Skye?"

"Yeah?"

"Someone's here to see you."

Whiskey would be a good enough reason for my mouth to go dry, but that didn't account for the catch in my breath and the squeak in my voice. "Oh God. Stuart?"

She nodded.

"Oh here we go again," said Gonzo. "You know what? I'm going to go snoop around while you play footsie with the dead." He turned and walked across the street again without looking back.

I followed Frannie's gaze and tried to face where Stuart might be standing. Or floating. Or whatever ghosts do. Fairies I'm used to, but ghosts aren't my thing.

"S-sure, for a little bit, I guess?" said Frannie to the air.

"What? What's he saying? Minnie, can you see or hear him?"

"No, Skye," whispered Minnie in my ear. "You and I are one, and I only live in your world and the fairy world. Not Shadow."

Frannie listened for a minute, then said, "It's a loan only. No funny stuff. I can push you back out just like that!" She snapped her fingers, putting her other hand on a curvy hip.

She turned to me. "Um, it's easier this way. At least for him. Okay, Skye?"

"What way, Frannie?"

She took a deep breath, sipped at the spiked Big Gulp and set it down. "The more direct way."

I held up my hands, palms flat toward her. "No. No way. No freakin' way!"

She took a breath and closed her eyes.

I held my breath.

Frannie's mouth broke out in a goofy grin. "Hey babe. I heard you like girls now. What do you say?" She winked.

I knew that grin, I knew that wink. I knew that body language.

"Oh Stuart. I'm so sorry. So, so sorry!" I threw myself on Frannie's body and sobbed. "I thought you h-hated me, and I thought Queenie s-stole you, and then it was t-too late." I bawled and made incoherent noises, soaking Frannie's t-shirt in the process.

"Aw crap. It's been what? A year? More? Hard to tell from over here. But one thing about over here is it's calmer. Usually. Skye, I'm the one who tossed the damn sword hilt to you. I knew what I was doing. Stop the waterworks, okay?"

"B-but Ernie, he said he saw you! And he said you're upset!"

"And the Night Duke would *never* lie to benefit himself, hmm? He got that far in the game because he's ruthless, Skye. He jumped on the chance to 'marry' you in the game as soon as you were available. He *uses* people, Skye. But yeah, I was upset. Not at you. At him. He's being stupid. Super stupid. Major league stupid."

I pulled back and wiped my eyes with the back of my hand. Frannie's sand-colored eyes weren't the same as my Stuart's, but the sad, tender look in them was all him.

Annabelle, please forgive me, but I've missed him.

He reached up to brush tears from my cheek, but stopped and stared at Frannie's hand. He laughed. "You know that expression about knowing things like the back of your hand? This is freaky, seeing her hand instead of mine. Where's that girl even *get* glow in the dark glitter nail polish? Love the Avengers ring, though."

I laughed, and said, "At least you're about the same height and build."

"You do like 'em short, don't you? Your firefighter is a little hellion of a girl, isn't she?"

I bit my lip. My head swam. No, that's not right. Not my thoughts, but my emotions roiled inside me in chaos.

"Oh Skye, I'm sorry. It's okay. I approve. I mean, wow, you did great. You know I love you, but if she makes you happy, that's what I want for you. Doubt Fran's gonna let me borrow her bod to let me sex up my ex anyway, right?"

"Not your ex. Not exactly. We never officially broke up, Stuart."

He closed Frannie's eyes. "Well, I did tell you to piss off."

"I get that now; it was to save me from what happened to you. To keep me safe from Queenie."

He shook his head. "Maybe so, but it was shitty, and I made it happen, it wasn't you. I'm glad you moved on, Skye. But this soap opera stuff isn't why I'm here."

He looked somewhere over my shoulder and said, "I'm getting to it, hold on!"

"What?"

"Frannie wants me out, soon. No time, sweetie. Look. You figured out Ernie's up to no good. But he's not the only player on the field. He's got something that should have stayed lost. An artifact. But now it's found, and it's gotten too close to something that can use that artifact's power to break loose. You gotta stop him, Skye, or he's not just going to hurt a few people while he gains in power, but he's going to free something that will hurt, maim, kill and destroy everything in its path. Maybe even rip down the barriers between worlds."

"But Stuart," I said.

"And you have to use your *head*, Skye, not just that bit of magic steel at your side. I think in this case, it'll cause more harm than good. I can't foresee what's going to happen, but it's not going to be as simple as it was with Queenie."

"No, you don't understand," I said.

"I'm here to try to get *you* to understand, Skye. Be very careful, and stop Ernie before it's too late."

"You idiot," I said, kissing Frannie's mouth.

I've had some weird kisses in my time, but this one left them all in the dust. My first impression was of the taste of cola and whiskey and the stickiness of her lipstick, a slight chill to her lips. I wanted to feel Stuart in there somewhere, but had no response. And then, he kissed back, through her lips. His spirit made her arms hold me in a strong embrace, and I melted. I forgot all about Frannie, about Stuart's death, and even for a moment, about my girlfriend. Lost in time and worlds, Stuart and I reunited for one more kiss.

And then it ended. Her arms went limp, and so did her lips. Stuart had left, and now I kissed my friend Frannie. For a long, strange moment, neither of us moved, but we remained in an embrace. I admit I was more than a little afraid to move. Maybe she was too.

I heard tiny giggles right next to my ear. Some big shoes scuffed on the pavement not far away.

Frannie and I sprang away from each other. I wiped at my lips, to remove traces of her lipstick. No, I don't know why.

Minnie slid down my arm and rolled in the grass laughing.

Further away, Gonzo stood gaping at us. I don't think I'd seen the big guy speechless before.

"What are *you* looking at, jerk-face?" said Frannie, turning away from Gonzo and me.

"I accept bribes in liquor," said Gonzo.

"Bribes?" Frannie said it at the same time as me, in the same tone.

"Sure. You wouldn't want Jimbo or *especially* Annabelle to know what I saw."

Frannie laughed but didn't turn around. "Jimbo might actually get a kick out of..."

I slapped Gonzo. Hard. I balled up my fists and glared up at him. "It was Stuart, okay? I was kissing Stuart. Not Frannie."

Shadows hid Gonzo's eyes from me. He stood still, arms at his sides. "And that's better how?"

"It just is, okay? I got him killed, so I owed him that much thanks. Tell Annabelle. I don't care. Maybe she'll dump me. She's working up to it anyway, I think. Sick of supporting me. Sick of me getting fired. Sick of the fairy world and pretend vampires and everything about me! So *don't lecture me, Gonzo!*"

The echoes of my voice came shrill and loud to my ears as they bounced back from nearby buildings.

Gonzo rubbed his face where I'd hit him. His words came slow, one at a time, and with a slight drawl. "First of all, I was joking with you. Second, don't you *ever* hit me again. And third? Goodnight. It's been fun; we should do it again sometime. Really."

I reached for him, to stop him, but he flinched away and Minnie yelled at me. "No, Skye, don't!"

Frannie's hand touched my shoulder, to hold me back. "Just let him go, you've done enough, okay?"

"I'm sorry, Gonzo," I said, and all the beer and whiskey and emotions of the day caught up with me all at once. The world spun and wobbled, no one had pretty auras anymore, and I had no idea what to do next.

As he stomped off, Gonzo called over his shoulder, "Go home, both of you. There's nothing there, and Skye's too drunk to find her ass with both hands. You're not taking on a football team of trolls tonight. And if you do, I'm not bailing you out, 'cause I warned you. See you tomorrow."

Chapter Nine

I'll be honest here. I don't remember the trip back to the hotel. Oh, I remember flashes, I guess. There was this horse with a horn, hitched to a carriage. I think I had a conversation with him. An argument, because he said he wasn't a unicorn, even though he had just one horn. And gargoyles crawling all over the glass structure of the Artsgarden. I was relieved when they didn't chase us. I swore I saw Annabelle in the crowd, but she was too tall, and wore a My Little Pony costume. Annabelle hates My Little Pony. Oh and I remember the part where I threw up in the street in front of Steak n Shake. That memory's pretty vivid. I hit the sewer grate, I think.

The next thing I recall, I stood naked in an unfamiliar shower, fighting off high pressure pulsed bursts of near-scalding water. I grabbed the single handle and turned it. And screeched as icy needles rained down on me. I jumped sideways, taking the shower curtain and rod down with me with a terrible crash. My elbow struck the toilet seat, hard, through the shower curtain and I cried out.

"I thought you were a pro at this, Skye?" Frannie's voice came from above and behind me somewhere. I rubbed my elbow with my other hand and twisted in the tangled mess on the floor to see her.

She blocked her view of me with one hand. "First you're kissing me, now I've got to see you naked? Do I have to remind you I'm straight?"

"Remind yourself, doofus!" I giggled at my comeback. Sometimes, the things that come out of my mouth are pure genius.

"Look, what happens at Big Con stays at Big Con, okay? Come on, I'll help you up."

I also don't remember standing, or the rest of that shower. I lay on my bed in the hotel room, wrapped in a towel, my hair laid out on a hand towel draped over my pillow. I put a hand over my eyes. "Too bright, turn out the light. Hey, I'm a poet and don't know it!" I laughed.

Frannie sighed. "Let's get some sleep, Skye."

I sat up in bed. "Wait, I need my phone!"

She propped herself up on one elbow and stared at me. "Why?"

"Gotta say night to my Belle!" I stood up and grabbed at my towel as it tried to slip off me. I congratulated myself on being clumsy but fast.

Frannie covered her eyes with a hand, just in case. "I don't advise that, Skye. If you're in the doghouse already, calling her when you're shit-faced isn't going to help things."

"Who's shit-faced? I'm all clean now, see?" I put my arms wide to show her, but lost my towel.

"Skye…"

"Clothes, right." I rummaged around in the drawers and came up with my FFF costume. No. A bra. Not for sleeping. A Heath Brewery T-shirt. Perfect. Panties that said "Oops" all over them? I put them on and laughed.

"Now what? And thank you for getting dressed."

"Nothing, just remembering."

Pleased with this accomplishment, I found the switch to the lamp and the room plunged into darkness. All I had to navigate by was the digital clock radio and a flashing smoke detector light. My feet tangled in the unseen damp towel on the floor and I fell on Frannie, who cursed at me and shoved me out of her bed. I sat on the floor and cried.

"I'm sorry, Frannie. I like you," I blubbered. "You're a good friend. Thank you for helping me. I'm sorry I'm such a screw-up."

"You had too much to drink. I blame Gonzo as much as you."

I thought of Gonzo's face after I slapped him and bawled.

"He's pissed at me," I wailed.

"Yeah, he'll get over it when he sobers up. Don't try to keep up with Uncle Gonzo. He's twice your weight. Just go to bed, it'll all work out in the morning."

I sniffed and nodded even though I knew she couldn't see. Standing up seemed like a risky move at the moment, so I just hauled myself into bed without standing. It took a couple of tries.

Not wanting to figure out how to get under the covers, I rolled myself up like a burrito in the comforter. The room did a slow roll around me. My ears buzzed. I had another thought. "Minnie! Minnie!"

No answer.

"Minnie! Minnie!"

"What now, Skye?" Frannie's voice came out as a tired whine.

"I don't know where my Minniekins is! She doesn't answer!"

"I'm sure she's fine. You're too wiped and trashed to go looking for her anyway."

"I sure hope she's okay. She's me, you know. Only littler and smarter and funny."

"Mmmhmm. Nite Skye."

"Nite Frannie."

The world slid away from me, replaced by thick, deep darkness and a growing roar, like the ocean inside a seashell.

* * *

The power line felt thick and warm to the touch as I clambered over the street, so very high up. Only the pudgy little hands I saw weren't my own, nor were the stocky little legs that I felt wrapped around the massive cable. Even through the insulation, I could *feel* a disturbing hum of electricity, like pressing a hand against a glassed-in beehive. I was Minnie. Well, I saw things through her eyes as I slept. I tried to call out to her, or make her mouth say words, but Minnie seemed unaware of my attempts. I'd just be a passenger on this trip.

Minnie inch-wormed her way along the line, and though my mind reeled at the heights, she moved with confidence toward an enormous brick building. As she neared a cluster of wiring where the line entered the building, she let go her legs and dangled by her hands. If I had the ability, I'd have screamed.

It was best that I couldn't. Minnie swung her feet forward and back, forward and back, in greater arcs until her toes nearly touched the cable. On the next forward swing, she let go her hands. My screams should have been heard for blocks around, but no one could hear but me. Minnie did a tight underhanded somersault as she dropped, then stuck out her feet and put her arms high above her head. The spinning slowed, and her feet planted on a ledge a couple of Minnie-heights below the power line junction. She gripped the brick mortise with her fingers and stood there breathing for a minute.

I had no clue she could do these acrobatics. She climbed crabwise along the bricks until she came to an archway. She clung there, peering over her shoulder, waiting for something.

Something turned out to be one of the trolls. A big one. It marched out of the night, into the pool of streetlight at the side of the building. It marched, eyes forward, hunched over, grumbling. No blue sports jersey adorned this troll, but a drapery of canvas tarp over his rust-stained limestone body. The movements of his limbs made a creak-groan-THUD noise with each step.

Minnie took a deep breath as he approached, and I thought she worried he'd hear her breathing.

But no.

As the immense creature passed under her and into the archway, Minnie let go of the bricks and pushed off, tumbling through the air to land an impossible distance below on his tarp-covered back. She gasped and slid, and just as I thought she'd waited too long, she grabbed two handfuls of tarp and dug in her fingers. Claws sprang out of the ends of her fingertips, and she clung fast to the heavy material.

The troll stopped just inside the doorway and scratched his head with a nasty grinding noise. Minnie held her breath again. The troll spun around, causing the tarp serape to billow out. Minnie's head passed within inches of the side of the arch, and she pulled into a little ball, clinging like a tick.

The massive stone creature whirled the opposite way, his joints creaking like tectonic plate activity. Through Minnie's eyes I watched the bricks approach at a dizzying speed, and I had to hope I hadn't peed the bed in fear. Minnie twisted, and like me in my blanket burrito back in the hotel room, she rolled up in the thick canvas garment. Her backside whacked the bricks, padded by a few layers of the heavy material. I felt the wind whoosh from her lungs. Still, those surprising claws of hers held fast.

I heard a THUD, THUD, THUD, pause, THUD, followed by a few heartbeats, then a clank and a drawn out rusty creaking of ancient hinges. From inside the folds of the troll serape, Minnie and I saw a brick door swing open, lit by flickering orange firelight.

Our troll spoke with an unseen troll, inside the doorway. I didn't catch what was said, only the impression of another language or an impenetrable accent, growled at a register almost too deep for Minnie's tiny ears to make out.

Creak-groan-THUD. Creak-groan-THUD. The troll strode forward, and the brick door shut behind us, melding into the wall surrounding without any evidence of a seam or hinge. Just a massive brass handle marked its location from the inside. The flickering firelight turned out to be an old railway lantern, like a silly toy in the hands of the other troll, even though he seemed head and shoulders shorter than the one Minnie rode on. I had another terror grip me as the guard watched the bigger troll pass by, but if he saw Minnie wrapped in the canvas, he gave no sign.

We descended stairs on the back of the troll, whose head scraped the curved brick ceiling. Down and down we went, at least three or four floors worth of stairs, far under the streets of Indianapolis. The stairway darkened, then brightened as we passed occasional torches in recesses in the wall. The brickwork gave way to mortised stone walls and soon after, the troll's descent ended in a stuffy cavernous space. More brickwork made arches everywhere, and shadowed tunnels marched off into the subterranean dark.

Our troll grabbed a torch from a rack and lit it off one at the bottom of the stairway. It flared and guttered and then brightened the area around us. The troll thudded its way down one passage, turning this way and that, through larger rooms and nearly crawling through low tunnels. Water dripped from the ceiling now and again, the drips splashing off his canvas serape and hissing in the torch's flames. Several drips formed a thin stream that ran down the furrows in the canvas and down Minnie's back, chilling her spine, which caused her to shiver and shake.

The troll stopped again, stock still. I heard a "whuff, whuff, whuff" noise, like a large dog panting. The troll's head swung around, and the noise repeated. He was sniffing the air.

"Who goes there?" came his boneshaking voice.

Minnie's heart thudded in her ears and I wished I could rush to her rescue, Fairy Hilt blazing. *Don't get eaten, Minniekins!*

The torch blazed a bright fiery arc as the troll whipped it around to light up shadowy crevices and corners nearby.

"I smells a rat. Er a narsty leetle spy. Come out er I'll roast yer gizzards on me torch while yer watch!"

I felt Minnie's little fangs prick the skin of her lower lip, shaking with fear. Her lungs burned with an ever more insistent need to take in breath.

The torch lowered to the ground.

BOOM! The troll slammed its stone hands together, knocking the held breath from Minnie. Another clap BOOM and she gasped and let go. Minnie slid down the canvas and tucked into a roll as she hit the dirt floor below, coming out of it in a frantic, scrabbling run into the darkness of a side tunnel. Stone scraped on brick as Minnie-sized fingers grasped after her and she let out a wail and fell and rolled. She rolled faster, battered against bricks, spinning out of control, until her head whacked a stone wall. Like an out of body experience, I watched for a moment as her body tumbled out of sight, down into the recesses of the tunnel, and all faded to black.

Chapter Ten

I woke to music. Tinny, jangly, hooting music assaulted my pounding head. Sunlight filtered through my closed eyelids, eclipsed here and there by quick shadows. The floor thumped with feet pounding along with the music's beat. Frannie's voice sang along with the pop song, adding to my poor head's pain.

Still cocooned in blankets, I rolled away from the light and sounds and fell off the other side of the bed with a whump, face first into the scratchy hotel carpet. I heard someone whimper, and realized it was me.

I struggled with my linen restraints, but only ended up rolling to the nearby wall. My arms pinned, legs bundled together like a mermaid's tail, I only managed pathetic flopping around. I could ask Frannie for help, but my pride forbade that. My pride and I wormed around on the floor, dragging blankets and sheets off the bed with me as I propped myself against the wall and pushed with my feet.

Frannie cavorted around the room, arms and legs flailing, red hair thrown this way and that. I had a weird impression that it was a tribal ritual or some terrible spell meant to raise the dead. She sang along with the music blaring from her phone. Then she noticed me. She laughed. "Oh Skye, I should take a picture."

"Do it and die," I said, giving her my worst skunk eye.

Still laughing, she danced over to me and tugged at the blankets while I struggled, not wanting her help. A few minutes of this freed one of my arms and I shooed her away and pushed at the blankets, emerging from the Skye-rollup like a newly formed butterfly with a hangover.

"What are you doing?" I asked as I stood up from the pile of blankets and sheets at my feet. I straightened my over-sized T-shirt and pulled it down to hang at mid-thigh, enough to cover my underwear.

"Dancercize!" said Frannie, grinning.

"I didn't realize you exercised," I said as shut my eyes against the sunlight streaming in through the parted curtains and rubbed at my temples.

"Didn't use to, but when you've been partly dead, you want to take better care of yourself, you know?"

I confessed that I didn't know that and rummaged around in my bag for aspirin and my toothbrush and toothpaste. A family of tribbles had taken up residence in my mouth overnight, and I needed to clean out what they'd left behind.

My hand hovered over the light switch to the bathroom, but in an act of self-preservation, I left them off. I could see well enough without them.

In the mirror, a willowy Medusa stared back at me. I grabbed a ponytail holder and pulled the masses of wild snakes into a choke hold and tied them back. One or two sprang up to menace me, but all I cared at the moment was about brushing my teeth and spitting without hair getting in the way.

After I did that, I took the aspirin and drank four little hotel tumblers full of water. *Should have done that before bed.*

Rather than take another full shower, I turned on the tub faucet, freed my Medusa hair mess, and dunked my head under the running water. I'd left it tepid, rather than hot, since my hair would thank me later for the cool rinse. Not quite cold enough to be a shock, but still soothing, the water spread out over my scalp. I imagined it washing away the headache and soaking into my body through my pores to help cure my dehydration.

I must have crouched there rubbing at my head and wringing my hair for longer than I realized, because Frannie joined me in the bathroom and flipped on the light. "You gonna live?"

I shut off the water and wrung out my hair. "Go 'way. I'm still partly dead, like you said."

"Come on, dry your hair, get dressed, and we'll get some breakfast."

Frannie took over the bathroom for a bit and I threw on a bra, a breezy green sundress with a Celtic knot pattern, and my sandals. I found the Transit King's gift on my nightstand and I put the tiny flask around my neck, facing the MacLeod family crest outward. I grabbed my backpack and stuffed things I might need later in it: the Fairy Hilt (why did that nag at the back of my mind?), a few granola bars, my flask of vodka, some jeans and a random T-shirt in case I needed to change, my Fantasy Free Form costume, and my purse. And a water bottle for refilling later.

Once she was ready, Frannie led me out of the room, down the elevator and into the hotel's restaurant. My stomach rebelled at the aroma of food, but the knot of hunger overcame the wave of nausea. I spied someone with coffee and I must have stared like a creeper, because she gave me a dirty look and turned away from me.

Frannie took my arm and led me to the buffet.

We feasted. Frannie had a fruit plate and some oatmeal. I had eggs, bacon, toast, orange juice, coffee with cream. Each bite restored a bit of my humanity. Each sip of coffee gave me some of my strength back and drove back the headache.

"What time's your shift with FFF?" asked Frannie.

Something nagged at the back of my mind. Something urgent.

"I'll have to check my phone, I forget." I rummaged in my purse inside my backpack and came up with a dead phone. *Great.*

I found the charger and plugged the phone in and turned it on. After it started up, it chirped several times as text messages rolled in.

The first text said it was sent a bit before midnight. Annabelle sent, "Are you there, love?" The next few were spread out over a few hours, also from her: "I'm home now," then "Getting ready for bed. Hope you're okay, Skye," then finally at about a quarter to 4, "Goodnight. I hope you're safe in bed, and not in trouble."

I sighed. "Stupid phone, I missed a bunch of texts last night. Annabelle's not happy with me."

Frannie blushed. "Sorry. If I'd been sober, I'd have reminded you about ghosts. They drain batteries." She tapped her phone. "I have to keep mine in this metal case to shield it. Still have to plug it in several times a day."

I frowned. "How far do I have to stand away from you to keep that from happening? I kinda need my phone."

"Well... probably five or six feet. I can help with that, though," she said, eyes lowered to her empty plate, fingers fiddling with her silverware.

"What do you mean, can you tone it down?"

She shook her head. "I can, well, um... it's a little strange to talk about, but I can move away from my body a bit, away from you. If I do, my reactions slow down, and I'll seem a bit dull."

"Hmm, well, I don't want to put you out. I can charge often if you're around."

She shrugged. "I'll do what I can, okay?"

I nodded and went back to the other messages.

Early this morning, Rebecca had checked in with a cryptic message. "Give me a private call as soon as you get this. RB."

Who signs their text messages? My badass bosslady, that's who.

"Gotta make a call," I said. "Can you pretend not to hear?"

She smiled and as an answer, poked at her own phone.

Before I could pull up Rebecca's contact info to call her, my phone rang as I held it.

Annabelle.

I picked up and chirped, "Good morning, sunshine!"

Annabelle drawled, "Sunshine? Are you *still* drunk?"

The tease hit too close for my comfort and stung more than she meant. I said, "Nope, but I could go for a mimosa right about now."

Silence for a few heartbeats, then she chuckled. "Yeah, I bet. What happened last night?"

I decided that partial honesty was my best policy. "We got threatened by trolls; Gonzo took us drinking so we could stalk them. A bit too much too fast."

"Yeah, and?"

"Well, Stuart's ghost possessed Frannie to warn me about Ernie, and I got all carried away and weepy and Gonzo yelled at me and I slapped him and he stomped off."

Long silence this time. "Jesus, Skye."

I babbled on. "Then we went back to the hotel to sleep it off. Oh and my phone battery got drained by Frannie's ghost."

"You nerds sure know how to party," she said. I wished I could see her face, because her tone gave nothing away.

"I miss you," I said. "I wish you could be here."

"Yeah, me too. I could party with you, or at least keep you out of trouble."

I laughed. "I don't think even you can do that. Trouble's my business, babe."

I heard a smile in her voice. "Is that your new catchphrase? 'Cause I know it's not original."

"It's not?"

"Don't get me wrong, love, it's cute. Just..."

"I know. Just be careful. I'll try harder."

"You better. I know big burly guys who'd jump at the chance to sit on you in shifts to keep you in one place, out of trouble."

I let my voice purr as I said, "Oh really? I didn't realize we'd reached that stage of our relationship. Screw the con; I'll take the number 34 bus out to party with you at the firehouse."

"Bitch. You're not supposed to call my bluff."

I grinned. "You should know how I am by now."

"I do, that's what I'm afraid of."

"Sorry I didn't call. You got it right; I was trashed and passed out without checking."

"It's okay. Just try to check in more while you're on supernatural spy missions for me, please?"

"Yeah. Bosslady wants the same; she's next in my queue to talk to."

"I'll let you go, then. Love you."

"Love you too, my Belle."

We hung up and a text came in from Phil: "Dealer hall opens in 10 minutes. Where are you?"

"Crap," I said aloud, standing. My battery said 12% charged. It'd have to do.

Frannie stood too. "Time for work?"

"Yeah, I'm running late. I feel like I'm forgetting something important."

"You didn't check in with Rebecca," said Frannie.

"I know, I know, I'll talk to her on the way."

Frannie trailed behind me as I swept out of the hotel and across the street to the convention center.

"Tell you what, Skye. I'll run on ahead and stall Phil while you call her and change."

I smiled and patted her shoulder in thanks. She gave me a big fake wink and peeled off on her own.

I dialed Rebecca and she picked up instantly.

Rebecca spoke in a stern but hushed tone. "Skye. You didn't check in. What's happening?"

"Yeah, sorry, it got a little crazy. There's more than one weird thing going on at the con. One of the gamers in my group, Ernie, has some kind of power, probably a magic item in the form of a hat. Lets him influence others."

"Influence how?"

"He has a couple zombie slave girls following him around."

"Zombies? He animates the undead?"

"No, boss, they're alive, and they wake up if he loses the hat, even for a moment, but they go back into a trance as soon as he puts it back on."

She paused a few heartbeats. "A magic hat? That will take some research. Doesn't ring any bells. Could be nasty, but I doubt it's what I sensed. You said there was some other supernatural activity?"

I told her about the troll confrontation and threats. I almost held back about our stupid stakeout, but I told her anyway. Something about Rebecca made me want to spill my guts.

"MacLeod, you're reckless. It's best that you got sidetracked. I told you not to engage, just observe and report. Got that?"

"Yes ma'am," I said, in a small voice. I pushed my way through convention crowds to a ladies' room to change into my Fantasy Free Form costume. The time on my phone said I had about a minute. *Not gonna happen, but Phil will forgive me. Having two bosses kinda sucks.*

"Uh, Rebecca, I gotta change and go help out Phil."

"Yes, of course. I will see what I can turn up on trolls, chains, and the hat. Good work, MacLeod."

"Yeah?" I entered a stall and started pulling off my jeans.

"Well, other than the reckless behavior."

"I know, the Force is strong in me, but I'm not a Jedi yet."

"I'd say not. But we'll work on that, young padawan," she said, and I could almost hear her smile.

Yes! She does have a sense of humor! "Bye bosslady."

"Stop calling me that. Check in soon." She hung up.

I struggled out of my clothes and into the costume. I banged my elbows and a knee in my haste in that small steel stall.

I peed too, because even tardy shield maidens must heed nature's call.

Hands washed, backpack slung on my shoulder, I faced a vast herd of con-goers shuffling by inches into the dealer hall, which had just opened for the first day of the con. Some comedians made mooing noises.

I reached the doorway after a week or two, or so it seemed, and was stopped by a Star Trooper. "Badge?"

Crap!

I stopped and crouched to rummage in my bag, earning some curses from a pileup in the herd behind me. I came up with my dealer badge and put it around my neck.

Satisfied, the Star Trooper waved me in. "Move along, move along."

The crowd inside plodded along at a maddening pace, and I bumped into people at every turn on my way to the Fantasy Free Form booth.

Phil scowled at me as I arrived. Frannie stood handing out postcards with the FFF logo and QR code. She shrugged and smiled.

"Sorry, Phil, you wouldn't believe the night I had."

He shook his head. "Try me."

I gave him a winning smile. "Ladies don't tell all their secrets," I said.

He nodded. "Yeah okay. Let me guess, your other boss has you running?"

Close enough? "Pretty much. Had to do some investigating, my way."

"Oh, your way, hmm? Does it involve a 'little' help?"

A little help? Oh he means Minnie.

"Holy crap, *Minnie!*" I said, loud enough to startle some passing gamers.

Frannie and Phil both turned to me and said, "What?"

My dream came to me in bits and pieces, flashes of brick walls and dizzying acrobatics.

And a grasping giant troll. And Minnie tumbling into darkness.

Restless Spirit

"Minnie's in trouble! I have to go help her!"

Chapter Eleven

"What? You just got here," said Phil.

"I'll make it up to you. I'll work another shift," I pleaded.

"This is opening hour on opening day! It doesn't get bigger than this."

"Skye," said Frannie, "What's going on?"

I recapped the dream I'd had last night for them. Frannie nodded throughout, but Phil's scowl deepened.

"Look," he said, "You and I have been through a lot of impossible stuff, but isn't it a simpler explanation to take that as just a dream?"

I shook my head. "No, Phil. I've seen through her eyes in dreams before. She's in trouble."

Phil sighed and walked over to the table to demonstrate his video game to a curious person standing nearby.

"But what can you do against a troll king," said Frannie.

As if to make up for my plan to run to help my other half, I grabbed up a pile of postcards and handed them out to everyone who passed with a grin. "I don't know, but I can't leave her there alone. I can't believe she tried that by herself without talking to me first."

"What will you do? Just walk up to City Market and ask for the secret troll lair? Then what? Shout at trolls until they give her up?"

"I said, I don't know! If only I could sneak in like Minnie, unseen somehow."

I had a sudden idea. "You're right, Frannie, I don't know what I'm getting into. I can stay here a bit longer if you can do me a favor?"

Frannie sighed and closed her eyes. "You want me to Casper my way over there and look for Minnie? It's not really that simple, Skye."

"Why not? Does it hurt?"

She shook her head. "No, but travel in the shadow world isn't mapped to our world. I have to find a focus I'm familiar with, preferably with an emotional attachment, and cut through. Once I'm there, it's much easier to navigate by following souls I know than to just move in physical space."

"Fairy space is weird too, I guess, but not like that. Can you find her, do you think?"

Frannie shrugged. "I can try. The trolls are fairy, so they shouldn't have any power over my spirit, but I don't think I can go into actual fairy space. So it has to be a real physical location or someplace in Shadow or I can't follow her."

"Please, could you try, Frannie?"

She nodded. "You'll have to babysit my body though. I'm not all there without my ghost."

I smiled. "Hey, you babysat me while I wasn't all there, barfing in public."

Her lips twitched upward at the corners, and she locked me in eye contact. "Yeah, so you owe me a couple times over. Take care of me while I'm gone."

"Of course!" I posed with my toy sword like the heroine I pretended to be for FFF.

She sighed. "Now, I gotta figure out how to get close."

"I hate to bring it up, but I bet you have a strong memory of that place across the street where I—"

She cut me off by putting fingers on my mouth. "Shhh. I'd prefer to forget that, Skye. But yeah, that'll work. Bye for now."

Her eyes, still on mine, lost focus, stared through me, past me. I turned to see what she looked at, but only saw the crowd shuffling past the booth.

Her hands fell to her side and her features relaxed. For all the world she looked a little stoned.

"Frannie?"

"Hi Skye," she said, eyes half-lidded.

"That's still you?"

"Yeah. Some of me."

"What's it like?"

She shrugged. "Like napping, kinda. Only awake."

I shivered. She reminded me a little too much of Ernie's zombie thralls. "Do you need to sit down?"

She shook her head.

Phil handed me more postcards. "Come on, if you're not leaving, make yourself useful."

He did a double take when he saw Frannie standing there in her dumb state. "What's with her?"

I didn't feel like weirding Phil out even further, so I punted. "Uh, long story. Call it astral projection, if you like. Means I can stick around a bit while she finds where Minnie went."

Phil glared at me. "Just how much weird do you think I can swallow?"

"I am not kidding you. Look, I'm handing out postcards, looking sexy. 'Cause otherwise, I'd run off to go look for Minnie myself."

Phil frowned. "Do what you have to, but thanks for sticking around a bit."

And I did my best. I turned on my Duchess Sofia persona from the vampire game, all sensual charm and flirtatiousness. My high wattage smile and skimpy costume drew in the gamer guys, mostly, though I flirted with a few of the girls and most appreciated it.

I posed for pictures with a *lot* of people. I hammed it up, posing in fierce or sexy ways. I made people laugh and smile and they lined up for demos of Fantasy Free Form. Phil gave out T-shirts to those folks, and talked up his digital baby.

I overheard whispers among passing people, saying the game was dangerous. I overheard the word "coma" more than once.

The whispers didn't stop the demos, and no one bothered Phil or me about it. I did see one or two people point at Frannie standing slack-faced nearby. I had to keep an eye on her, whether it slowed business or not.

But my flirty performance overcame any misgivings people had. They wanted to talk to me, they wanted to be seen near me, and if I'm being honest, they wanted free FFF T-shirts.

Time flew past. I enjoyed the extroverted high of interacting with all my fellow gamer types, I loved being the center of attention, and I welcomed the distraction to take my mind off of Minnie's predicament and whatever Ernie and the trolls might be up to for a little while.

I guess more time passed than I'd realized, because my stomach rumbled and Phil took a break to get us some food from the trucks outside. I had the booth to myself. Well, other than Frannie, who reacted if people talked to her, but did nothing active.

The crowd thinned a bit, the initial rush of opening day having worn off a bit, but the Skye Show still had a crowd clustered around thick enough to block the aisle.

I felt like a star. Phil had called me "a natural" earlier, and it all went to my head.

Mom always told me role-playing wasn't good for anything. She should see me now!

Phil took awhile, and my stomach complained about this. Frannie had sat down, her hands clasped, a placid, vacant look on her face.

A commotion, some kind of cheering, approached. A big group of gamers, walking together, made its way down the bigger aisle. Some kind of parade? A celebrity?

Ernie led a contingent of blank-eyed people in zombie costumes and makeup through the dealer hall. The two girls from Heath's preceded him, carrying a banner that proclaimed, "Join the Zombie Walk! Tonight at 8 near Hall J! Brains!"

Ernie wore that top hat, and had added a flowing black cape that clasped with a tarnished bronze brooch with a bear's face on it. He directed the zombie parade with a polished wooden walking stick that had a silver head. It reminded me of an antique table leg, other than the topper. He led a troupe of a couple dozen zombies, mostly attractive women in grisly costumes. Right behind him marched two massive zombie guys. The guys sported renaissance gear and gruesome makeup.

Looks like Ernie got some bodyguards. I guided a couple of people to the lines for playing demos, then stepped out in front of the parade.

"What do you think you're up to, Ernie?"

The girls never broke stride as they body-checked me. I stumbled and the bodyguards shoved me out of the way.

I hit the floor in a sprawl. The zombies marched along; one girl stepped on my fingers, another kicked me in the side and fell over me, then got up and kept walking.

I spied that table-leg walking stick and grabbed on and pulled hard. Ernie joined me on the floor in a lanky pile of elbows and knees. I smacked my forehead into his, and though it hurt, I accomplished two things.

First, Ernie lost that smug grin on his face, went cross-eyed and let out a yelp.

More important, that stupid top hat flew from his head.

I yelled in his face, "Got you now, jerk!"

Ernie snarled and shouted, "Get her!"

Rather than being freed by me knocking off the hat, the zombies continued acting zombie-like. All of that parade stopped their march and turned, staring right at me.

Oh crap! I kicked Ernie in the gut, knocking the wind from him.

I scrambled backward into the crowd surrounding the Fantasy Free Form booth. Several helpful hands reached down to lift me back to my feet. Nervous applause broke out among my fans.

Except the zombies advanced and grabbed the front ranks of the FFF crowd. After a quick protest, those grabbed twitched and thrashed around, then joined the crowd, blank-eyed and coming for me.

I backed up further, warning the bystanders, "Watch out, they'll get you too!"

Chuckles rippled through the nearby crowd, thinking this all part of an act.

They're getting assimilated because of me! I've gotta get out of here! I dodged toward the tables and around some slow-moving zombies, and into the wider aisle ahead of the original parade path.

The two goons that had shoved me before advanced, hands reaching and grasping for me. I danced and dodged, distracting them from the other bystanders. I had no other plan, so when I backed into a knot of people at an intersection, the burly zombie guys caught me. Their meaty hands locked on my wrists and they held me in place between them. I struggled and yelled. My wrists burned with an icy sensation, something familiar and terrifying about that touch.

I flashed back to the possession, being filled with cold fire and blackness, when my body hadn't been my own. Because I'd given up my rights to it, once upon a time.

But not this time. I'd been there, done that, and the demon had been banished and I'd been warded against anything like that happening again. I'd reclaimed my rights, I'd barred the door.

I screamed for help.

Ernie appeared before me, bent over and clinging to his walking stick, gasping for breath.

"What's wrong with you?" I shouted at him.

"Release... her..." he hissed, teeth gritted, eyes smoldering.

The big guys let go, and the icy assault on me stopped too.

In my peripheral vision, I noticed Frannie stand up, her eyes wide. She took a step toward me, then another. I wanted to warn her off, but I didn't dare look at her, for fear of drawing attention to her. I couldn't protect her from this many zombie people.

Hell, I can't protect myself. Gotta break his power over them somehow.

"What's this all about, Ernie? Can't be about the vampire game."

He stood straighter, but still leaned on his walking stick. "Power, my dear. Isn't everything about power? Power in the game, money power, political power, sexual power... We all want to be in control, don't we?"

"And you've got some kind of magic to make people do as you say? It's evil stuff, Ernie, and this isn't a game. You're playing with a loaded gun. No, it's more like you're playing with weaponized anthrax. You're infecting people with evil magic, and for what? Kicks?"

Ernie shook his head. "You wouldn't get it, would you? I saw you there, surrounded by people. Think anyone's ever asked me if I'd let them pose for a picture with me, Skye? You've got your own power."

"Maybe so, but I'm not using whatever power I have to make people do something they don't want to do."

"Power's power, Skye. You're influencing them with your smile, your costume, those legs..."

Frannie took more steps, now mingling among the zombies. She blended well, moving slow and slack.

I thought fast and shoved Ernie in the sternum. He took a step back and fell into Raven, who caught him.

"There's always a bigger fish, Ernie. If I don't stop you, I know there's at least two other powers in this city bigger than you can dream. And your power doesn't work on *me*. That's one thing the black magic won't buy you. You can't have me, you bastard!"

Ernie swung his stick at me and missed. He held it point out at me to keep me away from him. "I could have you dragged off and tied up."

I sick knot grew in my stomach. *Hold fast, isn't that the thing?*

Maybe I'd have to bust out the wonderbooze sooner than I hoped.

"And bunch of people just heard you say that. And we're on Big Con surveillance cameras. If I disappear, who'll they come looking for?"

He looked up and around. "Maybe. But in awhile it won't matter. I don't need you, Skye, though it's a shame."

Ernie, the Night Duke, winked at me, a nasty, greasy wink. My blood boiled.

I saw red. I balled up my fists and braced myself, ready to launch into him to knock that leer off his face. Or some teeth.

Frannie grabbed the Night Duke's wrist and held a hand out to stop me. Her eyes focused on nothing in particular.

All at once, the air dropped about thirty degrees. I saw my breath. The Night Duke's eyes rolled back in his head and he sagged into Frannie's arms.

All around us, people dropped to the floor, marionettes whose strings had been cut at the same time.

"Skye, I can't do this long. Get the hat."

"It's not the hat! It must be something else. What is it?"

"I'd look, but this takes everything to fight. It's on him. Pick something."

I grabbed the walking stick away from Ernie's limp grasp.

Big Con security chose that moment to show up in force. A couple of Star Troopers and a bunch of men and women in neon green VOLUNTEER shirts pushed through the crowd to the edge of the pile of unconscious zombie people.

Frannie and I stood in the middle of that pile. I looked at her. Her eyes cleared and focused on me. She bit her lip and let go of Ernie and collapsed.

It seemed like a good idea, so I fell down, too, clutching that walking stick.

Chapter Twelve

After we hit the floor, some people further away groaned and began to rise. I overheard them talking to security, confused and disoriented.

I stayed down, playing possum.

A hand shook my shoulder. "Skye! Hey Skye, are you okay?"

I cracked an eye open and saw Phil hovering over me, worry all over his face.

He noticed and dragged me away from the pile. I let him, as part of the act, so security wouldn't blame me for this mess.

"Phil, don't say anything, but go get Frannie, too, if you can," I murmured.

He leaned me against the booth wall and looked me in the eyes. He opened his mouth to speak, then nodded his head and went after Frannie.

The pile roused, most people standing and talking to each other. Some backed away and disappeared down the aisles of the Big Con dealer hall.

If Ernie still lay on the floor, I couldn't see him in all the confusion. Phil emerged from the clamor, leading an exhausted-looking Frannie by the hand.

She said, "Skye, we'd better go. I'll explain later."

Phil frowned. "Go? And leave me by myself?"

She gulped a few breaths before looking at him. "Phil, this is bad stuff. We gotta go."

He nodded. "Okay. I think I'll be okay for awhile. But take your lunch, okay? Got you a burrito from the Taco Wagon." He handed me a paper sack.

I took it and hugged him. "You're safer without me here at the moment anyway."

He sighed and went back to the demo table to talk with some people who just arrived.

Frannie took my hand and said, "Get me away from here, Skye, I'm fried."

I led her through the crowd, keeping watch for Ernie, his goons, or Raven and her friend Donna. We exited the dealer hall and I took her up an escalator. I spied some small presentation rooms, and found an empty one. I closed the door behind us.

She plopped into a chair and put her head down on the table. Her shoulders rose and fell and she shuddered and I realized she was crying.

"Hey, Frannie, it's okay!"

I sat next to her and took out a foil-wrapped burrito. It was cut in half, so I offered her half. "Come on, eat something, you'll feel better."

She sobbed a moment longer, then sat up and wiped at her eyes. "Sorry, I got all scrambled and drained back there."

"What did you actually do, Frannie?"

"I went looking for Minnie, and when I returned, I found you surrounded with zombified people. Outside of my body, I saw a network of... I don't know, smoky tentacles, I guess, all coming from Ernie. Only I couldn't see him through this cloud of black stuff. Made me think of the demon, you know?"

I knew. I nodded and hugged my arms around myself against a sudden chill.

"I tried to oppose the blackness, but needed to get close, and I couldn't do that without my body. You had his attention, and I used that. So, I tagged along behind as I had my body creep closer, unnoticed, until I reached him. When I grabbed him, it was as though I had my hands on a power line and it shorted out through me. My other part held on while I did that, but I had to stop, it hurt too much, and I was afraid."

"But you did good, Frannie! You freed all those people."

She shrugged. "For now."

I held up the walking stick. "And this?"

She shook her head. "That's not it. I'd know it if it was."

I cursed. "So it's not the hat, but it was before. How's it moving around? Couldn't you tell from outside?"

She shook her head. "No, it was all too dark just then. I don't see any dark on that thing; it looks ordinary, other than that silver doorknob on top. Can you keep that a little away from me? Thanks."

"Oh right, silver," I said, putting the stick on another table.

Frannie picked up her half burrito and inspected it. She picked off pieces of chicken and put them on the foil, and then bit into it, eyes closed as she ate.

I ate the extra chicken and started in on my half burrito. My stomach rejoiced. *Who knew facing down zombies could be such hungry work?*

After we filled our bellies, I spoke again. "So, what'd you find out about Minnie?"

"Couldn't find her. Since she's not of this world or Shadow, I had nothing to latch onto. But I did get to eavesdrop a bit. The trolls talked about some 'little menace' intruder that had the place in an uproar. They said the Chained Lord has a bounty on her."

Oh no, Minnie! "A bounty? Chained Lord?"

She nodded. "Some ancient troll who's in charge around here. He wants her alive. This tells me a couple of things. She's probably still in there, and that you and she are pretty important to this Chained Lord guy."

I said, "We gotta go after her, Frannie."

Frannie took a deep breath, let it out and looked at me with half-lidded eyes. For a moment, I thought her ghost had left her. She said, "Skye, I'll level with you. I can't help you. That thing, whatever it is that Ernie has, it's powerful, and I'd guess it's getting more powerful with each person that it pulls into its net. It's sheer Shadow energy, the kind of thing that saps life force. When I got caught up in it back there, I thought that was it, I'd go poof and be gone forever. That Frannie you babysat, she'd be it for me. I got lucky that time. I'm too exposed, all outside myself. I can't risk that again. I'll help however I can, but I can't go near Ernie and his horde."

I nodded. "I get that. But the trolls, they're fairy, not Shadow."

She sighed. "I know. And I'd risk it if I wasn't wiped out. But I need to rest and pull myself together."

I patted her hand, and met her eyes for a moment. "You've done so much already. Thanks."

"So what will you do?"

I shrugged. "Guess it's time to pay a visit to the trolls and find out what they really want."

"You're joking."

I shook my head. "Nope. I'm tired of sneaking around. No more riddles. I'm going to go and have a face to face with the Chained Lord and cut through the BS."

"But Skye, that's crazy. They could imprison you or kill you or who knows what!"

I smiled. "Crazy's what I've got going for me. I don't think they'll expect this, so I'll have them off their guard."

"You don't have the Fairy Hilt with you, what'll you do in a fight?"

I shrugged. "Even if I went back and got it out of my backpack in the FFF booth, how many trolls would I be able to take out before they got me? Five? Ten? How many are there? No, I'll just rely on fairy hospitality and manners, and if things go poorly, I always have the wonderbooze." I patted the tiny flask hanging on its chain around my neck.

"What's that going to do for you?"

I grinned. "I don't know! But it'll be fun finding out, I think."

She shook her head. "Skye, maybe we should find Gonzo—"

I cut her off. "No. I doubt he's in any mood to talk to me, seeing as he never came back to the room last night. It's best I do this alone. Wish I had some iron, though. I miss having a fireplace poker by my side."

"Iron? Hang on." Frannie rummaged around in her purse and came up with a handful of rusty nails and poured them into my hand. Each was about as long as my middle finger and quite thick. The head showed more rust than the rest, so I guessed they'd been used.

I stared at her as though she'd just pulled a rabbit out of a hat. "How in the world did you get these? They'll do fine!"

"Don't you remember? Last night, in our drunken travels back from our stakeout at the troll lair, we passed by a storefront that had renovations going on. After the thing at Monty's, everyone in a football jersey made me think of trolls, so I wanted protection against fairies on me. I saw those lying around and grabbed them up."

I grinned and tucked the nails into the waistband of my skirt. "Uh, the trip back was a blur. That's genius though, thanks!"

I stood up, and she did too.

"I think I'll try to find Gonzo anyway," she said.

"Tell him I'm sorry, and he gets one free shot on me."

"A shot of whiskey or a shot at slapping your face?"

I sighed. "Either. Both."

"It'll be okay. He's forgiven worse."

I hugged her. "Be careful. I'll check in later."

I left her there and made my way through the convention crowds, down the escalator, and out on the street. As I left the convention center zone, the packs of gamers thinned out. I passed what had to be the renovation site where Frannie had gotten the nails, and vague memories came back of needing to pee while she rummaged around there last night.

Then I realized a flaw in my plan. I needed a drink or two, and my flask was in my backpack in the dealer hall with Phil.

So, I made a detour to Heath's. I found the place overrun with gamers. People stood around outside, some even had broken out colorful collectible card games or dice to make a game of the waiting.

I don't have time for this.

I wiggled my way in and found a free seat at the bar, between a Star Trooper and some guys dressed in some adorable My Little Pony costumes. I saluted the one, and fawned over the others. The Star Trooper returned my salute and the bronies preened at my compliments.

"Back so soon?" Greg Heath slid a mug of dark beer in front of me.

Have I mentioned my love for this man? He's the best.

"You're a mind-reader, Greg!" I cried, toasting him with his own beer.

He held fingers up to his forehead, concentrated, and said, "Skye MacLeod. Skye MacLeod." He then pretended to read something written on his hand. "How does Skye talk when she's had too many beers? Skye MacLeod."

I laughed, almost choking on the big gulp of beer I'd been downing.

"Careful with that stuff, it's Black Hole Porter," said Greg.

"Black Hole Porter?"

"So dark, not even light escapes."

I laughed again and my vision took on a fuzzy quality, a sign that I began to see two worlds superimposed on each other. "I can feel its gravity."

"That too. It started out extra high gravity, so it's stronger than anything on my chalkboard right now."

I believed him. This stuff might not be the magical gruit, but it made up for that by being bold and strong.

"Good stuff. Got any more gruit?"

He shook his head. "Gamers drank me out of the stuff last night."

"But you have some special reserve?"

He shrugged and grinned. "Maybe, but not on tap."

As the strong beer settled into my system, I noticed things around the bar I hadn't before. The bronies next to me had actual equine heads and hooves for feet. A cluster of tiny gargoyles sat among the salt and pepper shakers. One of them slurped up some spilled beer on the rubber mat by the taps. The others waited their turn. Then I saw the trolls. Big rocky guys stood in the waiting area; one seemed to resemble limestone, the other red brick. They played rock-paper-scissors with each other several times, then one hung his head and the other pumped a fist in triumph. The droopy red brick troll thudded toward me.

I downed the rest of the Black Hole Stout. "Got anything stronger, Greg? I have to leave in a hurry."

Greg followed my gaze and said, "Trouble?"

"Yeah. I'll be okay, but I need something for the road."

Heath came up with a small, flat, swing-top glass bottle. "Can't sell this stuff, medicinal purposes only. But I can give away a sample."

I slipped the glass flask into my other back pocket, eyes still on the trolls. "Thanks, Greg."

Before the brick troll could say anything, I said, "Okay, boys, take me to your leader."

Chapter Thirteen

The two rock-heads stood there gaping at me for quite a few beats before *thanking* me for cooperating with them. Such courtly fairy folk. But I remembered the fairies trade favors as currency, and no matter how rotten they might be they always keep the letter of their word. Catch one in a blatant lie or breach of contract, and you own their butt. They've got other obsessive-compulsive traits that set them apart from humanity, but this sort of absolute honor is the best thing to know when dealing with them.

I offered to buy them drinks before we left, but they refused. Not to be polite, but so they wouldn't owe me anything, I suspected. Except they already did. I saved them an expected fight. I made their jobs easier. Since I'd flashed the Hilt yesterday, they all knew I had power beyond ordinary mortals. My reputation for killing an evil Fairy Queen last year had to make them worry about taking me on directly.

That reputation could be a sort of currency as well. I hoped so, anyway.

Heath raised an eyebrow as I talked to the big guys and I smiled and shook my head. The bronies scuffed hooves on the bar room floor, nostrils flaring, their gorgeous colorful manes flipping to and fro. *Guess if I'd needed allies, I'd have been in good shape.* I flashed my smile and waved to them and they whickered and flipped rainbow tails and went back to their drinks.

The golf-ball sized gargoyles had vanished.

Brick led us out of Heath's and through downtown. Limestone followed behind, a little too close for my comfort. He seemed apologetic about it when I griped, but I guess they thought I'd make a break for it. Maybe a smart person would. I needed to save my Minnie and get to the bottom of at least some of the weirdness going on around me. As we wandered around town, the further we got from Big Con, the fewer bits of the fairy world I spotted. Oh, sure, there were some pigeon people cooing around some statues, gargoyles here and there, dozing on ledges, and many tinier flower pixies swirling in the wind above traffic. But to see truly alien and flamboyant fairy creatures, you needed to go to Big Con. Any gathering of oddball humans draws the fair folk, cloaked in mundane illusions. At a place like Big Con? Fairies let their freak flags fly, and everyone applauded them for original cosplay.

I wondered as we plodded on toward City Market whether gamers had some inherent fairy quality about them, or whether fairies were just drawn to the imaginative gamers. The Transit King had told me that I had traces of fairy blood, from clan MacLeod intermingling with fairies hundreds of years ago. A lot of what the Transit King said ranged from fables to pure bullshit storytelling. I doubted he'd claim relation to me without meaning that though. Fairies took family trees *very* seriously.

As we passed Monty's, a cluster of fairy folk, along with a few Star Troopers, watched us pass. I made out a two-headed cat-man, three duck-people, and a swarm of those nasty little blue flame sprites. Lucky for Monty the flame sprites stayed outdoors. I'd had my house burned down by the little buggers.

But no one called out, and no one stopped our march. The Star Troopers disappointed me. Surely one of them had seen what happened yesterday, had heard the threats made against me. Maybe even had been one of those knocked down by the trolls. But then, they couldn't see the troll-nature of these guys. I squinted and saw that their glamours didn't include football jerseys today, so I guess that explained that.

But the fairy folk? Well, they owed me nothing, and they're a remarkably self-serving bunch. They served one purpose though. My visit hadn't gone unnoticed. If I disappeared, word would get out. And in the mortal world, Frannie knew my intention, and even sort of the location.

We passed through a more powerful glamour around City Market, one that seemed to make the eye point anywhere else, to avoid looking at the brick door Minnie had gone in overnight. Hidden in plain sight, mortals would avert their eyes, find other things more interesting to look at, even feel uneasy enough to go somewhere else. Since I had a buzz going, I could see it for what it was, and I could push back against the effects. That, and the burly trolls kept nudging me back on course.

I wondered how well a direct assault would have gone last night if even I had trouble approaching. I had a funny image of Gonzo turning one way, Frannie another, and me finding distractions galore, unable to focus on the real entrance.

Minnie could have shown us the way, I suppose. But as confused as we'd have been, that troll guard just inside would have an enormous advantage, and could have run to warn others before we got halfway down that long stairway.

Maybe Stuart showing up was the best thing that could have happened. I mean, yeah, here I was going in under a white flag, with no weapon but a pocket full of rusty iron nails and the mysterious Wonderbooze, but at least Frannie and Gonzo wouldn't be risked too. That and my dreams from Minnie gave me insight on the layout of the underground tunnels.

Brick pounded on the wall. My skin still crawled with the go-away enchantment, my gut told me that I'd rather be anyplace else than here. The invisible door's outlines appeared, shadows deepening in the cracks, then it swung open with a gritty moan. The foyer was as I'd seen it through Minnie's eyes, only this time, I saw the guard. A smaller troll, made of shiny black obsidian, fixed his eyes on me. I'd expected a big, rocky oaf like my escorts, or the ones that'd faced me down at Monty's. Not this guy. His glittering eyes held a quick intelligence as he scanned me from head to toe. His mouth pressed into a line, and he extended a thin, sharp blade to point at me.

"Why is she not bound?" His voice hissed and gurgled like volcanic fissures.

Brick deferred to Limestone, who said, "She's unarmed. She doesn't have *it*, Sarge. She *asked* to see him."

Sarge fixed me with those sharp, beady eyes again. "Why have you come?"

"I didn't come to talk to *you*, buddy. I came to talk to the Big Kahoona. These gentlemen were good enough to escort me."

Gurgle, hiss. "Tell me, fairykin. Why are you here?"

Fairykin? That's a new one on me! "Look, I've got business here. These guys would have collected me anyway, am I right?" I turned and looked up at Limestone. "Think he wants to be kept waiting?"

Limestone looked from one troll to another and then back to me, shaking his head. "Yeh, we best get on, awright Sarge?"

Steam leaked from Sarge's nostrils. He let out a huff of air and stepped aside without a word.

Down and down and down the winding stairs we trooped. At the bottom, each troll grabbed a torch and lit it, lighting our immediate area. The far walls lost in shadows, all I saw were archways and support pillars marching off in all directions.

"Don't yer try anyfin," warned Brick, and I realized I'd started to lead the way Minnie had gone. I dropped back.

"Hey, it's cool, I'm just anxious to meet the boss, you know?" I flashed him one of my winning smiles.

His brows knit in a corrugated stone frown. "Yeh, sure. Who inn't?"

Limestone guffawed at that.

I followed Brick down passages that looked more familiar when I turned to peek behind me. When we reached the point that Minnie had run off, I tripped myself, on purpose. I cursed, because the landing hurt. I hoped that made my act more convincing.

"Hey, yer awright? Careful, lil fairykin, er the big boss'll throw hisself a fit if he thinks we roughed yeh up."

"Ow, crap I'm clumsy. Hard to see down here. My foot hit something." I peered down the side tunnel while I nursed my knee. *Wish I'd changed out of this silly skimpy costume before going on this little adventure.*

Down the passage, which seemed too low for my two companions, low enough that even I'd have to stoop, I saw smaller passages still branch off of it off in the distance, at the limits of the trolls' flickering torchlight. No sign of Minnie, however. Just in case, I slipped one of the iron nails out of my waistband and tucked it in the bricks at the mouth of the tunnel, hoping the trolls didn't notice.

"Here, don't get it in yer head teh go down them old gobbo ways, girl," said Limestone. "Yer better off wif good ole trolls. Can't trust them lil gobbos. Nasty things. Get stuck in yer toes when yer not lookin'. Steal yer dinner if yeh blink. Troll might break yer head wiff a rock, but he won't mess wiff it and trick yeh into sellin' yer mum. Har."

"Har," said Brick.

"Har," I said, and they growled. *Note to self, only trolls get to say "har".* I pulled myself up off the dirt floor and brushed at the dirt and grit on my knees and elbows.

The trolls watched me, each letting out another couple of hars.

"Do I amuse you?"

Limestone nodded. "Yer a funny lil creature, yeh. I kinda hope he doesn't smoosh yeh."

"Yeh," agreed Brick.

I faked a laugh. "Come on, let's get this over with."

The trolls turned down another tunnel, one that went on and on. It might turn this way or that, but I saw no side tunnels or doors. We walked what had to be many blocks up on the surface, then came to another wide chamber. This one was lit from far above by shafts that pierced through the stone and earth, several stories up to the surface. The light that reached us had a bluish, wavery quality to it, rippling like water. I stopped there, waiting, staring up into that distant reflection of sunlight and sky and hoped I hadn't miscalculated and I'd never see the surface again.

Stop it, Skye, you're psyching yourself out. I peered around the chamber. Chains adorned the walls, thick enough to restrain an elephant. Open manacles dangled from the ends, also on a scale to hold pachyderms in place. *Wonder if the zoo is missing these?*

Solid wood doors big enough to serve as a garage for a Humvee dominated the far wall. A creak and a deep groan sounded from behind them. The trolls picked up wooden crooks and each hooked an iron ring on the door.

"Yer ready, lil thing?" said Limestone. "'Cause here's the Chained Lord hisself."

My heart thumped in my chest and my mouth dried out. I nodded, not trusting myself to speak.

"Har," said Limestone.

"Har," agreed Brick.

They heaved on their crooks and the doors groaned open, ushering a dank, cavelike earthy aroma into the chamber where I stood gaping.

Nothing but deep blackness met my eyes at first. A hole in space behind those doors.

Then a booming rumble that brought a lump to my throat, and I glanced around at the walls, the ceiling, at Brick and Limestone, terrified that the whole place was about to fall down on our heads.

Then, the rumble modulated up and down, rattling my teeth. It dawned on me that this terrible sound, a vibration I felt in my bones more than I heard with my ears, was a *voice*.

Speaking to me. I heard my name.

"Oh yes. Very nice. I have not seen the sun in lives upon lives, but the Skye has come to see me in my exile. Hoh ah ah ah."

Then, in the dark, two dim red slits opened, glowing like overheated iron. Eyes. But could eyes be so far apart? They rose up higher than my head, back there in the recesses of the blackness.

Every instinct in me screamed at me to *run*, but I stood frozen, unable to move, held by that impossible, terrifying gaze. "Come, fairykin hero. Talk with a lonesome old troll awhile."

Chapter Fourteen

My mind rebelled, icy fear numbing my feet and fingers. Wild panic gnawed at my ability to think and form sentences. But my body obeyed, my feet took small, slow steps *toward* the ancient terror in the dark. Maybe the Chained Lord's force of personality couldn't be resisted. Maybe instinct for self preservation understood the difference between hunter and prey; if I ran, I became prey. Until then, it was up for debate.

Either way, I shuffled forward, into the room, light fading with every step. A creak and groan followed as the doors shut behind me. The only light came from those burning slits of eyes. I had no idea what the Chained Lord might look like. I had only his *presence* to go on for his size. That sub-woofer voice, how far apart those eyes were and how high up, the feeling of pressure in the air all added up to one huge troll. Jabba the Hutt had nothing on the Chained Lord.

His breath came in long, languid gusts, like a blacksmith's bellows inflating and deflating in slow motion. I stood there, listening, counting five or so of my own breaths to each of his. In and out, in and out, it would have been hypnotic had I not been ready to pee myself in fright.

After a few minutes or days, he spoke, "I have heard of you, fairykin hero. Most impressive. But manners, manners. Let us introduce ourselves. Please, you go first."

I took a deep breath and cleared my throat. *Hold it together, I've got to hold it together, wetting myself won't win any points here.* "Your Excellency," I said, "My name is Skye MacLeod, a descendent of the Clan MacLeod of the, uh, Isle of Skye."

"Ho hah ah," he rumbled, "And some other fine blood, I suspect. I think you know of me, young knight, but indulge me, hmmm?"

I nodded. Unsure what he could see in the dark, I added. "Of course."

"I am the Chained Lord. Some call me the King Below, others say Troll Father. I had a name before I came to this, hum, this prison, but it has been forgotten by all but a very few. My role has become my name now."

"Like the Doctor," I said before I could stop myself.

"Hmmm?"

"Sorry, never mind, go on."

"Hah. Not a doctor, no. Once, I was a warrior king, so long ago. Before any MacLeod trod this continent, when the people knew and revered us as spirits of the land, I ruled. Those people understood the different realms so much better than the humans who swarm above our heads do now. You, on the other hand, have had a taste of fairy, as a result of a brush with Shadow, hmmm?"

"How do you know that?"

"Hoh oh, yes, how would I know, below the earth for hundreds of years, chained in this room? How do you know about times long gone? How do you know about places far away? I am told things, and I ask things, and my servants find the answers for me. And I sit and ponder and dream."

I took another few breaths, and then dared another question. "What do you want with me, your grace?"

"A good question. You might ask it of others. Like that grubby little upstart who rides carriages around the city above, as though they could be the straight tracks of old? Like the wife of his you slew with a most astonishing weapon. That weapon, almost as old as me, with power I thought long gone from this mundane earth."

A great clanking, clattering din of massive chains moving made me cover my ears. I sensed great power at work as the eyes moved toward me, one THUD, two THUD, three THUD as his steps brought him closer.

Then he stopped and hissed like a steam engine and groaned like railroad cars braking. The chain noise stopped with a shriek of metal on metal. Each link blazed with a silver light. Since my eyes had adjusted to the dark, the light burned, and I had to shut them. But not before a silhouette of the great troll had made a retinal photograph for me to see.

The Chained Lord crouched, back bent, knees as high as my head touched his elbows as he strained against chains fastened to the wall behind him. His massive chest could hold a Volkswagen with room to spare. That craggy head held nobility and terror, with a nose as long as my arm, eyes as big as hubcaps. In the fading afterimage of the Chained Lord, his jagged teeth frightened me the most, since that mouth could easily bite my head from my shoulders without any trouble.

Chains clanked, air whooshed as he sat with a great THUMP.

The Chained Lord let out a gusty sigh.

I opened my eyes, the outline of the troll still overlaid on the dark of the room, his fiery eyes fixed on me.

"Hoh hah, I am trapped as you see. But perhaps there is a glimmer of hope for me yet. Lady Skye MacLeod has a weapon of old, older than these chains that hold me, older than the enchantment that binds me. You have dealt with the gnarled little fool of the roads, you know of favors among our kind, hmmm, MacLeod?"

Favors are money, they're power, they're everything to these people.

"Yes, I understand how important they are to you and others of your realm."

The room rumbled, and I mistook it for a growl until he spoke and revealed it to be laughter. "Oh yes, to folk like me. But you are fairykin, are you not?"

Before I could answer, chains clanked and a great BOOM BOOM BOOM of his hands clapping together made me fall back on my ass. The glass flask of Heath's special brew, as well as a couple of my remaining nails, skittered off into the inky dark.

A crack of red torchlight sliced the room in half. The flickering line widened and the silhouette of a troll blocked some of the light. He carried something.

"Yer lordship," said Brick.

"Do you have it?"

Brick's shadow bobbed, "Yeh yer lordship. Lil nasty fing put up a fight. Used iron, it did. Heh. Ol' Obbie'll be limpin' fer weeks."

"Show her," said the Chained Lord.

Brick stepped in the room, carrying a torch and a cage. Inside the cage sat my Minnie, arms folded, her face screwed up in an angry scowl.

"Sorry, Skye," she said. "Thanks for the help, I tried but they got me."

"It'll be okay, I promise," I said.

"Careful with promises," growled the Chained Lord. "I don't appreciate sneaks and spies. But you may be able to help me, so—"

I interrupted the Chained Lord. Yeah, I don't believe it, either. "Really? You think you're getting my help by holding my friend ransom? If that's your idea of trading favors, you haven't heard all that much about me."

I searched around on the floor around me for the stuff I dropped. I might need those nails, and I sure could use that drink.

"Hooh hah hah, a bold knight indeed is the Lady Skye! Ransom? Oh yes, I could work things that way. I have *you* caught as well, and could bargain with your life as well as hers. Or is that the same thing? But no. I thought to give her back to you as a gift. A goodwill token, hmmm? To take back to the world above."

Fairies don't do favors for goodwill, not even my buddy Bask, the Transit King. Certainly not this subterranean terror.

I had an idea.

"In that case," I said, "In that case, I owe you an apology. And a gift, some hospitality in exchange for your hospitality."

Grumbles and chains rattling. "Hospitality? What have you? The sun to shine on my old skin? The hot breath of summer wind to caress my cold dank face?"

My hand found the small glass flask. "I bring a gift of small comfort. A sort of mortal magic, I guess."

I held up the bottle, and it glinted in the bright torchlight. Facets in the glass threw amber beams around the room like some medieval disco ball.

The Chained Lord rumbled and leaned toward me, eyes narrowing further. "What is this?"

"It is a brew, made by my friend Heath. He makes the finest beer in the city."

"Hum. Hmmm. A gift?"

"For you. No strings. I just don't want to seem ungrateful, your grace."

The room shook with the troll king's laughter. "Manners, ah yes, manners are not lost after all, it seems. Thank you, fair knight."

Brick set Minnie's cage down next to me. I opened the little door in the wire structure to let her out. Minnie climbed me and clung to my neck. I struggled to my feet, shoving the nails back in my skirt's waistband.

I took a couple of steps toward the monstrous king, holding out the bottle at arm's length.

Chains rattled, and the torchlight revealed a hand that could wrap around my waist and touch finger to thumb without squeezing me. Palm up, the hand waited. I placed the bottle in that hand and it slid into a great stone bowl of a palm.

"I wish I had something more to your scale, lord," I said.

"A gift is a gift, and I know of this brewer by reputation. It is precious to you, is it not?"

"It is," I said.

"Let us share, then, with no debts between us."

The hand disappeared, and though I can't imagine how he opened the swing top, I heard a pop, hiss and gurgle.

He reached back toward me and I plucked the bottle from between two of his fingers. Half of the liquid remained.

For the second time in two days, I toasted a fairy king. "To your health," I said, and tipped back the bottle.

Heath's brew had almost no fizz, and it filled my mouth with a sweet fire tempered by only a touch of bitterness. I forgot I was underground for a long moment, I forgot I stood before a creature who could squash me like a rat. I forgot Minnie, whispering urgent words in my ear that I did not hear.

In that moment, the dark fled, replaced by an amber monochrome, each object and creature in the room surrounded by a soft foxfire.

I looked upon the Chained Lord's face and smiled as the warmth spread from my belly out to my fingers and toes. He smiled back, a crooked, jagged grin so terrible that it made me laugh.

He laughed too.

Minnie trembled, clinging to my neck.

Brick backed up two steps.

"A delicious and potent beverage. I should like much, much more of this. Thank you for sharing a drink with me, scion of MacLeod. I foresee your name ringing out among your people's history."

"Aw, shucks," I said, riding the lovely tipsy buzz from the drink and the compliment.

"In good faith, I free you, fairykin knight, and your bold little squire too. I admire your courage. Bold you were to come into my domain without that weapon. If you return, come of your own free will, as my guest. And if you should like to be owed a great favor by a power beyond your imagining, then bring the Hilt next time, and break these chains."

For emphasis, he lunged forward again, manacles pulling chains taught. Only Heath's new brew allowed me to see things as they were, the light didn't dazzle my sight. A sort of geometric, crystalline aura surrounded the chains, and I thought I made out symbols, letters, numbers, all woven into the pattern. *Am I* seeing *a spell?*

"May I ask one more question, your grace?"

I saw him nod. "Very well."

"If I am to free you, I need to know why you were imprisoned."

Brick fled the room. Without the drink, I would have been blind in the dark, but the auras burned still.

"Hooh. My crime was losing a battle. I sought power, like all of us seek power. My armies fought to gain me a bit of power from shadow, to infuse myself with a bit of that world, so I could be master of three realms at once. Instead, my legions fell to an army of the dead, and since I could not be killed, I was chained here, under the earth, before your people came from over the waters and built the city and the mocking monument above my head. It stands like my tombstone, but I am NOT dead! I survive, and I dream to see the skies once again. I take your name as hope, pretty little knight. I hope your heart may take pity on this lost soul and let me free, next time we meet."

"Thanks for the answer. I'll think about it, okay?"

His fist slammed into the ground, his chains clattered, and the room shook. Or at least Minnie and I did.

"Good! Go from my tomb and think and dream and feel. Breathe in the air for me, Skye."

The doors opened again. I didn't need to be told twice. I said my goodbye and fled down the hall, leaving Brick and Limestone to chase after me.

Chapter Fifteen

I reached the surface through the blocks of twisty catacombs tunnels. I had to wait for Brick and Limestone to catch up before Obsidian would let me leave. He had murder in his beady eyes when he saw Minnie on my shoulder. A lump of reddish clay globbed on his ankle, he favored his other foot as he barred our way.

"This way is closed," he hissed.

Minnie hid in my hair, but called out, "The Big Guy says otherwise, slick. Move it."

He flexed claws and picked up a long spear that leaned on the wall next to him. "I take no orders from dishonorable iron-wielders."

"It's soooo honorable to hold people captive, hmm?"

Obsidian pointed the spear at me now. "More honorable than sneaking in on clothing like a flea!"

I held up my hands. "Hey. I gotta go. Your king says so."

He hissed again. "Once upon a king, maybe. He is our lord, but we are more his caretakers."

Minnie laughed. "Oooh, treason!"

"Not treason. Reality. Like the reality of you on this spear, spitted and roasted for a late night snack, if you don't shut your mouth."

I never thought I'd be so glad to see Brick and Limestone. They clattered up the stairs and made a show of getting on either side of me and Minnie, like they'd escorted us the whole way.

Minnie said, "Tell shiny-butt here to step aside, you guys."

"You can bite my shiny obsidian ass!" The point of his spear moved just inches from my face and Minnie's. I backed up into Limestone, and he caught me in an unexpected gentle hold.

"I would, but I don't want to chip a fang!"

Brick interposed, pushing the spear aside. "Oy, yer making somefing of nuffing. Boss says let the fairykin and the lil gobo go."

Obsidian's spear pointed at the ceiling. "That's no gobbo! She fights dirty, like a gobbo, but no gobbo could hold iron. Not even a gobbo'd sink so low."

"Nice folks, those goblins," said Minnie. "Sold me out, stink to make your eyes water, but still more pleasant than the likes of you."

I whispered, "Shut *up*, Minniekins. I just want to go."

She whispered, "Shh. This isn't optional. I wounded him, so it's this or a real fight."

"Oy!" snapped Limestone. "Shut it, all of yeh. Best rid of em, hey?"

Obsidian pulled himself to his full non-hunched height to stare daggers at Minnie. Then he looked me in the eye and said, "I ever catch her by herself, she's dead and in my belly. Orders from below or no. Got it?"

I nodded. "Understood. But just remember, she's under my protection."

We held the stare a long, uncomfortable moment, then he hunched back down and opened the door for us. Orange sunset-light glinted off Obsidian and splashed across the bricks behind him. The sweet evening air reached my face, and I took a long breath before stepping toward it.

Limestone's hand gripped my shoulder, stopping me short. He leaned in and murmured in my ear, "Mind yerself, pretty thing. Hate to see you squooshed. Boss needs you, yer fine. After that? Well, better watch yerself, that's all."

Minnie said, "She's not in this alone, blockhead."

I said, "Hush. That's a kindly bit of advice for a troll, isn't it?"

"Har. And blockhead's a friendly endearment. Weren't for the iron-handling, I'd wonder if the little one had a bit of troll in her."

Minnie made a raspberry. "No troll in me. I'm a special snowflake."

"You bet. Har. Now go, before you end up in someone's belly."

My stomach turned inside out and my brain wobbled like Jell-o as I passed through the obscurity spell on the doorway. The streets were washed in the bloody light of the dying sun. My shadow stretched out across the street, and I felt conspicuous, like it was an arrow pointing out, "Skye is here, come get her!"

Someone did spot me.

"Hey! Slappy McSlapperson! Over here!" Gonzo's voice rang out across the street.

Call it intuition, or maybe it was something in that special Heath brew I shared with the ancient underground terror, but the hairs on my neck stood up. I felt like a bullseye had been painted on my back. I looked over at Gonzo, standing next to a table on Monty's patio. A couple of other guys sat at the table. He waved me toward him. He wasn't smiling.

At the moment, hanging with a cranky Gonzo seemed safer than whatever had my alarm bells ringing. Gonzo might not be happy with me, but he'd keep me from harm.

"I'm heading over, Minniekins. Coming along?"

Her hushed voice seemed loud, with her riding right next to my ear. "Yeah, I'll hang out for a few, but I think I need to get back to scouting."

"Right. Haven't gotten in trouble in nearly thirty seconds, gotcha." It came out more bitter than I intended.

"Thank you, Skye," she sang. "I know you'll always rescue me. Just remember, works both ways. I may keep someone from frying your bacon someday."

"Yeah, yeah, I hear you, sis. Just keep out of trouble."

Her laugh jingled like sleigh bells. "Oh Skye, I'm part of you. If *you* keep out of trouble, I'll let you get away with saying that to me with a straight face!"

I let that go without comment, since Gonzo already thought I was crazy, I didn't need to reinforce that idea.

As I moved away from the hidden catacombs entrance, some of the anxiety ebbed. I thought for a moment that maybe I'd overreacted to the aversion from the protective spell around the entrance, but some persisted even as I crossed the street and joined Gonzo.

I noticed only a couple of trolls sitting around the patio area, disguised by fairy glamour. They watched me, but I didn't get the heebie-jeebies from these guys. I'd swear one of them was made of something like cinder block material. The other wasn't clearly a troll, could have been a very human-looking gargoyle, maybe some sort of angel statue come to life. They weren't close to Gonzo, anyway, and their interest only seemed watchful, no obvious evil intent toward me.

"Heya Gonz, I'm really sorry—"

He cut me off. "Forget it. I don't want to talk about it." The waning sunlight cast shadows, his eyes sunken and hidden from me, unreadable. "Skye, these are my biker buddies, Ham and the L.T. Guys, meet Skye. Met her in Chi-town, but she's a local here. Obviously one of the gamer dorks."

Ham shook my hand and smiled. I liked his milk chocolate skin, retro fro and outrageous sideburns. He stood nearly as tall as Gonzo, maybe a couple inches taller than me. I wanted to hold onto his hand, he had an aura of easygoing comfort that reminded me of my buddy Leslie.

The L.T. was shorter, buzz-cut, and had a pink scar in the middle of his forehead. His eyes scanned my skimpy FFF costume. More accurately, they scanned all it failed to cover. "Hell-o, nurse! Are you and Gonzo close friends?"

I wanted to kick him to make him look me in the eye. Instead, I said, "Sure, if my girlfriend and I ever get married, Gonzo's one of the first I'd ask to stand up for me as a bridesmaid."

"Bridesmaid! You mean 'best man'," said Gonzo.

I laughed. "Gonzo, sweetie, do you really think Annabelle'd be the one wearing the dress? You're on my side."

"Since when are you getting gay married? Can you even do that in Indiana?"

I shrugged. "Oh, we've talked, but we're a long way from there."

The L.T. said, "Ahhh, a *girlfriend.* Do you two mind if I watch?"

I'm not the slapping kind, I'm really not, but this guy deserved a good one. Gonzo caught my wrist on the backswing. "He's harmless, all talk, like a dog who chases cars. Wouldn't know what do to with you if he caught you."

Ham thwapped the L.T. on the back of his head. The L.T. lurched forward, and I took a step back so his nose didn't bury itself in my cleavage. He windmilled his arms to catch his balance, and Gonzo caught him by the shoulder before he fell.

"Bastards," said the L.T.

"Apologize to the nice lady," said Ham.

"For what?" He rubbed the back of his head.

"Just forget it," I said and turned toward Gonzo. "What's going on?"

Gonzo picked up a mug of beer and drained about half of it at once. He let out a champion belch that seemed somehow trollish. "These guys told me some stories you should hear. You in particular, you know?"

Ham and the L.T. looked at each other and shrugged.

The L.T. went first. "Well, I put my '74 Indian in the garage and walked over to the mall food court to get something to eat. There are these Goth girls dressed up like they're from that Walking Dead show. Hot chicks, but gross. I didn't want to like that look, but it did something for me," he looked around for support from the guys, then after a pause, at me.

We all stared at him.

I said, "Gross, why are you telling me this?"

He shifted around in his seat and stared at his empty beer mug. "Well, they caught me staring and came over and hit on me."

"Bullshit," said Ham.

"They did! They invited me to walk with them tonight. Real creepy-like, ya know? Like they wouldn't drop the zombie act for a second. They had these hungry eyes, I knew they wanted me, you know, at the same time, in some freaky necro-sexy acts."

Ernie's thralls. "Yeah? So what happened?"

The L.T. picked up his mug and let the last drop of beer roll down onto his tongue. He refused to meet my eyes. "Well, a guy has limits. When one of 'em touched me, I got all creeped out and panicked and ran off."

I nodded. "Limits are a good thing."

Ham said, "You bet they are. I saw those same Goth girls later in the afternoon, leading a bunch of guys by the nose. Some of the guys were here for the bike show, like us, and some were gamer types." He waved a hand in an arc to take in the Big Con types at tables nearby, and the Star Troopers standing around.

"Was anything strange about that?" I asked Ham.

He nodded. "Yeah. I mean, I know some gamers and I know they get into acting and all, but even the bikers had that glassy, nobody's-home look. I thought maybe it might be some kind of goofy flash mob until I heard the L.T.'s story the first time. Gonzo here said you're all into that X-Files stuff. What's going on?"

Honey, you wouldn't believe a word I said. I bit my lip and looked from Ham to Gonzo. The L.T. was back to checking out my cleavage.

Gonzo said, "It's okay. Ham here chases Bigfoot in his spare time. And the L.T. says he's been abducted by aliens. Twice."

The L.T. punched Gonzo in the shoulder. "Hey! That was between you and me! It's *personal*, man!"

A grin crept across Ham's face and he put a hand up as if to swear in court. "Guilty as charged. I want to believe."

I laughed. "If aliens came down and blew up the Circle Monument with a laser from the sky, right in front of a thousand people, Gonzo'd tell me it was a streetlight."

"You know what, Highlander? Screw you. I'm the opposite of Ham here. He goes looking for that paranormal crap, on purpose, and 'wants to believe'. It keeps finding me and I *don't* want to believe. But this shit's getting serious whether I want to believe in it or not."

"You're right about that. The trolls caught Minnie last night, and I just got her back. I've got a strange understanding with their big boss guy, and he's after me to cut him loose. I haven't decided if that's a good idea yet."

"Trolls?" said the L.T. and Ham in unison, a bit louder than I would have preferred.

I did my best not to turn my head and look at Cinder and Angel a few tables over.

Gonzo snorted. "Told ya you two were amateurs compared to Skye."

The L.T. cursed, but looked up at the sky, eyes searching. I thought I saw him twitch.

"So, these trolls, are they behind the whole Evil Dead parade?" Ham asked.

I shook my head. "No, that's something separate. Someone I know in the vampire game, he's got some kind of object of power that seems to be turning people into zombies."

The L.T.'s eyes couldn't open wider without his eyeballs popping out. "Like really undead, brain-craving walking corpses?"

"No, not like that. Just, well, hypnotized or something. Robotic. And under Ernie's command."

The L.T. glanced up at the sky again. "You sure it's not alien mind control tech?"

I laughed, I'm ashamed to admit. But really, how much more ridiculous is the idea of alien technology than a magic item infused with life-draining shadow powers?

The L.T. met my eyes, and I saw my laugh had stung him.

"Sorry. Trolls and shadow magic are way weirder than aliens. I haven't been through what you have, and you've only seen a bit of the scary stuff I've had to deal with. If you think of the shadow world and the world of the trolls as other dimensions, it *is* kind of like alien tech in that way. Just no spaceships, and the alien creatures from those dimensions are from right here, not far away. Just those places occupy the same space."

Ham said, "That makes sense."

Gonzo and the L.T. stared at him.

"Well, her explanation of whack-a-doodle stuff made sense."

I smiled. "Well, the trolls want me to set their leader free. Ernie just wants to gather up people for his own ego, as far as I can tell. But something worse is at work here, I can feel it."

Minnie stirred on my shoulder. "Hey! I said that!"

I decided not to answer her, since these biker dudes already believed way more than I ever dreamed. Adding that I have a vampire-like mini-me that lives in the fairy world might just be the bit of crazy that tips the scales into the bullshit zone for them.

"I want in!" said the L.T.

"In on what?"

"Whatever you got! Sounds like a fight or a bunch of weird-ass crap going down. You need help? I'm your guy."

Ham rubbed the L.T.'s buzz cut. "You're a good man, Charlie Brown. You know what? Crazy as it sounds, I want in too."

Suddenly, I've got a posse!

"Uh, great, but I don't even know what's going on yet."

"Sure you do!" said the L.T., his eyes bright. "You've got two armies. One's gathering today, the other's established. There's gonna be a fight."

Gonzo put up his hands, palms outward. "Whoa. Whoa. Slow down. The insanity here has just gone off the scale. Armies? We're not on either side. We don't know what the fight's about. Why not let 'em fight it out?"

"Because, Gonzo," I said, putting a gentle hand along his face, right where I'd slapped him. "If people get hurt because I didn't do anything to stop it, I'd never forgive myself."

Chapter Sixteen

So, we did what I always yell at characters in movies not to do; we split up. Minnie took off to go "scouting" again. I didn't dare shout warnings after her, not without drawing too much attention to myself. *Like the sexy warrior princess outfit isn't enough?*

Gonzo and his buddies said they'd do a few loops around the center of the city, within a few blocks, to look for other weirdness. The L.T. wanted me to come along with them, but I had business with Ernie that was best done alone. Dirty business.

They asked for my cell number, and I gave it to them, but my phone was still in my backpack, possibly still in the closed-and-locked dealer hall, and it'd been almost dead when I left it.

Damn. I ran off without everything important. No time to track down my stuff now, though.

I got quite a lot of attention on my way back to Big Con. I dashed around half the Circle downtown as the streetlights popped on. I'm a tall girl, so I'm used to getting looks, but in that little nothing of a skirt, my legs looked extra long as I ran. I'm not much in the bust department, but the girls bounced around enough to distract most men, and a few women, as I passed by at high speed. I don't mind a little attention, but right now, with that invisible target that tickled the back of my neck, being conspicuous meant danger for Skye.

A terrible thought occurred to me on my way to the rallying area for the Zombie Walk. *What if all that shadow energy, what if that mojo Ernie had was the demon returning to haunt me?* My skin crawled at the tiniest wisp of memory that came to me. I shoved that aside. The demon had been destroyed, or at least hauled back out of our world. It became a parasite attached to a poisonous host. The banishment made it scream like a cat being pulled through a two-inch hole by its tail. As horrible as that sound had been, it was that memory I clung to every time the possession gave me night terrors. Every time I feared I might not be alone in my own head.

No way is this the demon again. It's gone, it has to be! Ernie'd been himself, though strangely obsessed. The zombies lacked personality; no trace of intelligent malice lay behind those glassy eyes. Plus, the demon only inhabited a single host at a time, not this sort of contagious octopus of puppeteering. The chill of the energy involved gave it away as something shadow-related. That borderland between my world and the land of the dead couldn't be mistaken for anything else. Not if you'd been touched by it, like Frannie and me.

As I approached the convention center, I got fewer surprised looks, and more knowing smiles, probably from people who'd seen me in the costume in the dealer hall. The area buzzed with activity, excited gamers going to or returning from dinner after a day of fun. *At least, more fun than my day.* Between the chaos of the crowds and my head spinning with thoughts of shadow, I ran smack into a Star Trooper. I thought we'd both hit the floor, but he caught me, an immovable object to my irresistible force. His gauntleted hands held me by the biceps, then slipped around my back, pinning my arms.

"Help! Let me go!" I yelled.

The Trooper let go right away and pulled off his mask. "Damn it, Skye, it's me!"

Phil!

I just about climbed him like a stout tree as I wrapped my arms around him in a hug. "I am so glad to see you!"

Phil's cheeks turned pink and his Trooper gauntlets patted my back. "Uh, yeah. Hey. What's up with you?"

I let him go and landed on my feet and did a pirouette just for him. "It's just been a long couple of days of pissing people off, and it's good to see a friend. Besides, I might need backup."

"About that, Skye," he said. Pink deepened almost to red, and his eyes looked anywhere but at me.

Oh, right. Crap.

"Phil, about earlier—"

"Look, Skye, you got us a bunch of business, until Ernie came along and you ran off with Frannie. Had to shut down the booth for a bit after that, since Ernie got in my face and so did Big Con security. Ernie told them you'd started a fight. And it looked pretty bad, really, to most people watching."

"But Phil, I'm really—"

Phil held up a finger, and the pained look in his eyes stopped me short. "Let me finish, this is hard enough. You're kinda banned from the dealer hall, Skye. Which means I can't pay you for the rest of the con. Except maybe teardown, you can help with that Sunday evening."

He might as well have slapped me. "You're *firing* me, Phil? You know I didn't start it!"

He sighed and dropped his eyes to the floor. "You kinda did, Skye."

I will not cry, I will not cry! "Well, Ernie had those people enslaved with some kind of black mojo! You saw what happened after Frannie touched him, they all fell down."

Phil pursed his lips and nodded. "Sure, I know. But I can't afford a sales rep who can't be at the booth to sell. We're still a small company. I don't mean to be a hard ass, and it's not personal, Skye. But you can't chase after monsters for Rebecca and still do the job I gave you. I know it's important, way more important than me or my game, but I can't count on you, so yeah, I'm letting you go."

Not another *lost job! Annabelle is going to hate me.* Tears blinked out of my eyes and I wiped the traitors off my face. "I'm sorry. I really am."

He put a hand on my shoulder and soft, sad eyes met mine this time. "I know, and so am I. Look. You said you might need backup. What is it, how can I help?"

I took a few deep breaths, trying to hold it together. "The Z-zombie Walk. I've got to get to Ernie and stop him. He's making an army, Phil."

"An army? What for?"

I shrugged and shook my head. "I dunno. He's up to something, and people are probably going to get hurt. Like the people in FFF who we saved, Phil. It's that serious."

"How do you know?"

"They'll do whatever he says because of shadow energy. Frannie saw it. Shadow's the place between here and death. I'd bet anything the demon that possessed your game came from there, same kind of energy. This is pretty much the same sort of thing, except it's playing out in our world this time."

"Shit. A demon?"

"N-no, I don't think so. I think it's the same flavor of power those chicks who raised the demon used, though. I don't know how Ernie got this kind of power, but I have to stop him. Even if his plans aren't actual war like I suspect, he's *using* them, against their will. This isn't a game. It's no more consensual than the people who got trapped in FFF."

Phil ran gauntlets over his head, a dew of sweat on his face. "What can I do against something like that? I'm not Magtog, I can't cast spells. I can't swing a sword against people who're doing things against their will. How do you fight something like that?"

"Ernie's at the center, pulling the strings and he's the one wielding the bad mojo. If I can take him out, if I can get whatever he's using to do this away from him, it ends."

Phil nodded. "So what do we do?"

"At Heath's, when he lost the hat, he lost control of his 'helpers'. When I knocked the hat off him in the dealer's hall, nothing happened. Maybe it was something he'd hid in the hat that he has on him somewhere else? Maybe I can grab the real source of his power."

"Yeah, okay. But so what? If you don't know what it is, how can you take it from him?"

"If I can get close, maybe I can figure it out. Or talk some sense into him." I gave Phil a lewd wink and ran one hand down my waist, over the curve of my hip, and pulled the hem of the little skirt up an inch.

Phil coughed. "Really, Skye? You're going to hit on him?"

I shrugged. "Whatever works. Can you help me get close?"

He took a deep breath, then said, "If I act like security and someone complains, it means I'm kicked out too, and Fantasy Free Form loses a very expensive booth at Big Con. We put everything into this, Skye."

I nodded and sighed. "I've done enough damage, I get it. I'll figure it out, Phil."

"I didn't say I wouldn't do it." He smiled.

I hugged him again and planted a kiss on his scruffy, sweat-salty cheek. "You're a doll! Thank you so much!"

He gently pushed me away so he could look me in the eye. "Knowing that risk, I need you to promise to be more careful than the wild Skye you've been so far. Okay?"

I nodded. "More careful, gotcha. I can do this one sober, too. Drinking only gets me a look into the fairy world, not shadow."

"Good. But I may need a drink before this is all over."

"Got some booze in my backpack, along with some other important stuff," I said, tilting my head to one side in an unspoken question.

"Oh yeah, right. I gave your backpack to Frannie when she came back by."

"Awesome. Can you do me a favor and shoot her a text and ask her to meet me in about an hour at Heath's? And ask her to tell Gonzo?"

Phil pulled off a gauntlet and ripped his velcroed iPhone off his shoulder. He punched a button and asked Siri to do what I'd said.

As I stood there listening, someone collided with me. Someone short cold and wiry strong. I stumbled and grabbed onto the girl's shoulder to steady both of us.

Her stoned eyes stared into my neck. She growled and her hand locked onto my wrist. The room spun and wobbled, and a numb chill crawled up my arm, over my elbow and on up toward my shoulder.

"Leave me alone!" I shouted in the blood-painted zombie's face. The hot anger shot out from my chest to my limbs. That heat thawed my arm and made her jerk her hand away like I'd caught fire.

For a moment, her eyes cleared and fear came to them. "What? Where did you come from?"

I calmed a bit, cheered by this small victory. "Are you okay?"

"I don't know; I wasn't here a minute ago." She touched her face. "Oh no, I'm bleeding!"

"No, sweetie, it's makeup for the Zombie Walk," I said, trying to calm her.

"It's okay," added Phil.

She whirled to look at him, then around at the ranks of zombies around us. Then she ran off, the other way.

Phil looked at me, eyes wide. "What did you do?"

"I... I just got mad. It snapped her out of it, I guess."

"Keep that trick in your back pocket for sure," he said.

"Okay. It's almost time. Suit up and let's go."

"Yeah, that way if this ends badly, maybe I'll be anonymous."

"That, and no exposed skin might keep you from getting 'turned' too."

"Good point."

We rushed into the convention center, toward the vast space outside the dealer hall.

And we slammed on the brakes as we rounded the corner and saw it.

A sea of zombies faced us. Big Con gamers, people in business suits, others in biker gear, some in football jerseys, and even some scruffy-looking panhandlers made up the crowd.

The Night Duke's army stood easily a thousand strong.

Chapter Seventeen

Ernie stood upon a stage outside the main doors of the dealer hall. He spoke into a microphone. The two big football jersey zombie lieutenants flanked him. "Zombies, just a few more minutes and we walk!"

Silence.

"Cheer!" he cried.

As one, the crowd cheered "Yeah!"

"We can't get to him from here!" I said, pointing out into the sea of painted zombie faces.

"Wanna bet? Follow me!" As he waved his arm, I could imagine his fantasy character Magtog the mage, striding forward into battle.

Phil waded into the zombies, his bulk parting them like the Red Sea ahead of me. The zombies bounced off his black plastic armor and stumbled into other zombies to the sides, growling but not fighting.

"Cheer!" cried Ernie.

"Yeah!"

I stage-whispered to him, "I don't think he's seen us yet, Phil!"

"Don't get cocky," he grumbled, shoving his way through the thickening ranks of Ernie's thralls.

Hands grabbed at my hair, and I bit my tongue to keep from crying out. I stopped myself from kicking at the zombie's shin, but instead grasped his wrist in mine and locked eyes with him.

The businessman who held my hair drew in a gasping breath as I let my rage flow through me. He let go and fell on his butt. I offered him a hand and pulled him up to keep him from being trampled.

"Where am I?" he said, still in a daze.

I let go. "No time, just run. If someone grabs you, get pissed off. It works."

"But—"

"Do it, idiot!" I shoved him away from me.

Hands grabbed at him, but he pushed and shoved and waded back away, shouting.

I turned and saw that Phil had moved on, not noticing that I'd lagged. A few zombies closed ranks behind him.

Oh no you don't!

I let my anger burn on, and I grabbed one, then the other and pushed. I hoped the rough treatment would let them use their own anger, but I had no time for that now. I pushed past them and into the empty space behind Phil.

The stage loomed up ahead, and I saw Ernie staring at me. He licked his lips and said, "Grab her!"

Hands came at me from all sides, plucking at my costume, my hair, my face.

"Stop!" I yelled, and several of them did stop, eyes rolling in confusion. But more pushed past, walling me in.

"Ernie, I came to talk to you!"

The Night Duke's words dripped with sarcasm. "Skye, my beautiful vampire bride, how delightful of you to come visit."

I caught his eye, and he flinched.

I guess that rage had more use than just snapping a few zombies out of their trance.

"Just listen to me, Ernie."

As I hoped, Phil held his own, the plastic armor giving him shelter against the zombies' touch. He held a circle of the thralls off just by pushing them back one at a time.

Ernie took in a breath, then said, "Lift her."

Hands, so many hands, too many hands, grabbed me everywhere. As if in a mosh pit, the hands passed me overhead, and deposited me on the stage in a heap at Ernie's feet.

"Skye!" cried Phil, still too far to help, but wading step by step toward me.

I stared at him and shook my head twice and held up a finger. I got up on all fours, then rose to my full height, holding onto that rage as I glared at Ernie.

"I want a divorce," I said.

He laughed. "Aww, Skye, don't be like that. You're getting off the ride too soon; it's just about to get really fun."

I decided to change tactics. "Oh really? What's in it for me as the Night Duchess? Experience points? My own personal slaves? Don't think for a minute that I didn't notice the attempts to make me like these brainless thralls. I'm not the brightest bulb in the box, Ernie, but I can imagine what you'd do if you had that kind of power over me."

"Skye!" Ernie's voice carried to the nearest zombies, who repeated my name, and then more surrounding them heard and repeated. My name grew louder and louder as ripples spread outward into the hall, until there came a clamor of nothing but a thousand voices murmuring my name over and over.

I turned around and looked from zombie to zombie, eyes scanning the crowd. All eyes had turned to face us, mouths all around me, up and down the hall, all chewing on that one syllable in separate dissonance.

"Skye. Skye. Skye."

I couldn't see Phil anywhere near me. The faces moved inward, the crowd pressed tighter and closer. The chaotic babbling tuned in a little at a time, more and more of an echoing chant, until they synchronized as one mighty voice.

"Skye! Skye! SKYE!"

My blood froze and my skin crawled, and some animal instinct deep within me screamed at me to flee.

Instinct won. I whirled and ran straight into one of Ernie's goons. Like a wall of flesh and bone, the large enthralled man didn't budge, and I bounced off him. His lips spoke my name in time with the horrible zombie chorus. His arms closed around my shoulders in an absent but insistent hug.

I heard Ernie speak into the mic. "Stop it. Silence! It's almost time."

One final wave of my name babbled away into echoes and whispers, and then even the guy who held me shut his mouth and his arms dropped, freeing me.

I whirled, and I admit, I was pee-my-pants freaked out, but the urge to flee stopped cold, seeing no exits.

"Look, Skye, you're right. I hoped you'd join the party; I wanted to play with you. But nothing dirty. What fun is that, making someone do what you'd hope they want to do?"

"Ask these people. Is this what they'd want to do?"

He shrugged. "It's different with you. We're friends. You matter to me."

For the third time in 24 hours, I wanted to slap a man in the face, and this one deserved it more than any of them. Something stopped me. Sobriety, probably.

I need a drink, and not to see fairies. "Friends, yeah. So, if I were to join you? Walk with you without having to be enslaved?"

Ernie wet his lips and paused a moment, then said, "Would you?"

I took a step toward him, then another. My eyes traveled up and down his Ichabod Crane frame, searching for the source of his power. Not the hat. I had his silver-topped walking stick. My eyes slid off him though, when I studied hard. I had the same eerie feeling I had at the troll catacombs secret door.

A concealing spell?

I wished I had more of Heath's special brew, the one that let me see the spells on the chains that bound the ancient troll lord. I squinted and crossed my eyes in attempts to see past the illusion. I caught a glint of gold at his neck. Maybe a flash of red light?

Then a memory floated to the surface. *The clasp! He wore a clasp on his cloak in the dealer hall, some animal face with gem eyes!*

Ernie's eyes shifted around and then settled on mine, and I held them there as I took a step into his personal space, within touching distance.

His cologne made my eyes water, but I leaned in and said, "Sure, why not?"

Ernie leaned in, his face an inch or two from mine. His eyes watched mine. He turned his head and his eyelids drooped as his lips parted.

Oh God, he's trying to kiss me! My feet became ice, my stomach a cauldron of boiling lead, and so help me, I let him.

It might be my only chance to steal his black mojo.

His lips brushed mine, and I stood as still as one of the Chained Lord's gargoyles in the daytime.

Despite the risk of a single command from Ernie causing two thousand hands and a thousand mouths to pull me into bits, I took a grab at the spot at his neck where I could not look. My fingers closed around something metal and lumpy and cold.

His fingers closed on my wrist, His eyes popped open, and his slack expression clouded and reddened, a storm gathering behind his eyes.

I heard shouting far away somewhere, past the stage, past the zombies, out at the edges of hearing.

"Let go, Skye," he whispered. "Now. Don't make me have to go too far."

Chill shadow energies crawled up my arm like something alive, a downed power line washing over my whole body, and I trembled and shook and seized. My hand slipped from the prize and the Night Duke shoved me away from him, hard. I fell backward, out onto the mob at the foot of the stage.

Hands touched my skin everywhere. Hands, fingers, scratching nails, clammy palms, all over my legs and arms and back and bottom. I waited for the command from Ernie to the masses that passed me around in a rough parody of a mosh pit once more. The command could be anything, and these enthralled people, gamers, bikers, businesspeople and street people alike, they'd follow it. Just as they'd chanted my name over and over in unison, just as they handled me without thought even now.

Rage, if I could even summon it over the terror that paralyzed me, might not be enough against so many touching and grabbing at me.

A scream escaped my lips. I couldn't help it. I kicked out at the hands, I pushed at the hands, but more came in their place.

I tensed as Ernie spoke over the P.A. system. This could be it, I might die. Right now.

"Welcome to the Big Con Zombie Walk! Let's march, my undead minions, and show Indianapolis what we're made of!"

The whole mass of humanity turned as one and the floor and walls echoed with the sound of their feet clomping and shuffling together toward the wall of glass doors that led to the street outside the convention center.

The hands carried me as far as the doors, then I had less and less support and found myself sinking down among the horde of marching thralls. Lower and lower until the arms and heads and bodies of Ernie's slaves closed in over my head, and my feet touched the floor. My ass dragged on the rough carpet, and someone stepped on my left hand with spiked heels.

I cried out and shoved at them. Pain helped me find my rage, and I grabbed at bare legs under shorts on the one hand, and pantyhosed legs on the other and a primal scream tore from me, drowned in the din of marching feet.

The two I grabbed stopped and gaped down at me. Zombies pushed into them and carried them off through the door. Sneakers kicked at me and the anger boiled in me and I shoved and kicked and yelled and struggled to my feet.

I had no choice, rage or not, but to follow the march of the Zombie Walk as it spilled out onto the sidewalk and into the street. Tires screeched and horns honked, but the sheer number of people stopped traffic, and we swept past the food trucks. Heath's beer tent shook and collapsed, and the massed zombies just trod over it as another obstacle. Heath's staff fled the scene, and beer from upset pitchers ran on the streets like a flood.

What a pity.

The zombies spread out at this point, and I sidled my way through the moving crowd, seeking the edge step by step. I dodged the slow moving zombies and reached the edge of the march at last, free to dash away down a sidewalk of a side street.

My head spun, thoughts whirled and fought within my head. *Where are they going? What happened to Phil? What's Ernie going to do? Holy crap, Ernie kissed me in front of everyone! Where can I get a drink?*

More shouts came from behind me, and I watched as Big Con security plucked at zombie sleeves, ordering them, pleading with them to stop.

Heedless, the zombies marched on. I heard a ripple, a murmur, a roar come from behind, and then it became a mass cheer.

"YEAH!" The roar of the zombies' voices raised goosebumps on my arms and I froze in place. So did the security people.

The shuffling, stomping crowd only grew as it marched on. Security people, grabbed by cheering, glassy-eyed walkers took on the same look and gait and direction.

I saw police marching with the zombies.

Star Troopers arrived waving glowing laser sword props at the crowd, but were ignored.

Time to get out of here. I ran a block over and put my long legs to work, pounding the brick-paved street as fast as my breath allowed. I pushed past normal people on the sidewalks, dared to run across the street around honking cars, hoping to get ahead of Ernie's mindless army.

I peered down the next side street and found the middle of the march. I guessed that I'd gained a bit after the next block, and then realized their goal.

Monument Circle. It had to be. If I wanted to make a big show of something in Indianapolis, the Circle City, I'd march to the city's hub, around the Circle.

I heard the rev of an engine. Not the civilized vroom vroom of a car or truck, but the belching, barking sputter of a chopper.

Motorcycles!

I ran on down past Illinois Street, and caught a glimpse of the first few zombies flooding into the Circle around the Monument. Horses drawing carriages reared up and got out of their way. Cars stopped and honked, but disappeared behind the massed horde all too soon.

I hurried on toward the sound of the engines. *They're on Meridian. Hundreds of bikes. Run, Skye, find Gonzo!*

Night air tore at my lungs, blood pounded in my head, my legs ached, my chest heaved and I gulped in air to keep moving.

I burst onto Penn as black specks swarmed at the corner of my vision. I tripped and lost a sandal down a sewer as I smashed my toes into a curb. I fell and collapsed on the sidewalk cursing and gasping.

"Hey, it's that Skye chick," said a voice I knew. The L.T. loomed over me. Grinning from ear to ear, he offered me a hand. I took it, and he heaved me up and held me with an arm around my waist. He smelled like cheap beer and reeked of cigarette smoke. But his eyes focused on me, even if they crept a bit lower than my face, and he moved with his own free will.

I hugged him as I caught my breath.

"Zombies," I wheezed.

The L.T. leered at me. "Zombies?"

I nodded, breathing hard. "Circle. Zombies on the Circle."

"Yeah? What are they doing?"

"Taking over," I said. "Just like you said. An army. Growing every minute."

The L.T. nodded, all serious now. "Got it. Are they armed?"

I shook my head. "Just people. Slaves. Do anything Ernie says."

"Easy peasy," he said.

I shook my head, breath coming in slower gulps now. "Not easy. They're not volunteers. Can't hurt them, but they can hurt us."

"Why can't we hurt them?"

"Because it's not their fault. They're an army of hostages."

The L.T.'s face hardened and he peered up and down the street. "We need Gonzo and Ham," he said.

"Where are they?"

"Gathering the cavalry, babe," he said with a lopsided grin.

Chapter Eighteen

"Twenny twenny twenny four hours to gooo, I wanna be sedated!" Gonzo sang the Ramones song like a war whoop. I cheered, my arms around his waist on the back of his Norton Commando motorcycle. He revved the engine and we roared up Meridian Street at the head of a column of motorcycles. I guessed there must be at least a hundred of them rumbling and roaring behind in ranked formation.

I peered over Gonzo's shoulder, sputtering as I got a face full of flapping ponytail. Both of us wore retro bowl-shaped head protection that reminded me of World War II army helmets. The spire of the Soldiers and Sailors Monument rose up over 250 feet at the center of the Circle in the center of the city. I smiled at the encouraging figure of Lady Victory high atop the towering structure.

Below that was the rest of the Monument with its gigantic statues of Indiana pioneers and Civil War soldiers, wide steps and pools that could fit a couple of bathing elephants apiece. The steps led up to a broad circular stone platform.

The stairs and platform swarmed with humanity. Bodies pressed in, clamoring and climbing over one another, piling inward toward the stone structure of the Monument.

The outer mass of zombies crowded all around the base and into the surrounding brick-paved circular street.

"Ai oh! Let's go!" shouted Gonzo as they entered the edge of that circle, and my heart soared at the titanic roar of the motorcycles' engines that followed them. I raised my fist and let out a defiant scream! I shivered, goosebumps from my fingers to my toes.

Skye, hero of Clan MacLeod does her ancestors proud! General of a mighty army, doing battle with the forces of evil!

The L.T. and I had found Ham and Gonzo with much of this chrome-and-leather cavalry already gathering in the street on Penn. Gonzo had come up with a simple plan.

"If it's his voice that gives that dick his power, then we'll take his voice away from him. We've got some loud bikes here. If the zombies can't hear the pissant give orders, we cut off his power. Make sense?"

I laughed out loud with glee as the motorcycles started their first lap around the circle.

Abandoned police cruisers blocked the four streets around the Circle, lights flashing. The officers had been absorbed into the thousands that made up the zombie parade.

Gonzo had instructed the bikers to wear full leathers or at least long sleeves, gloves, and helmets to protect against the touch of the zombie people.

As they rounded the first quarter of the Circle, I spotted a row of Star Troopers with over-sized foam shields and padded mock weapons from the boffer arena in Big Con. The Star Troopers raised their weapons and beat their shields at the sight of the motorcyclists. I waved back at them. A larger Star Trooper saluted me and gave the thumbs-up sign.

Phil, I hope that's you!

As they passed the halfway point, I spied the Night Duke. Ernie sat hoisted on the shoulders of his goons. I saw his mouth move, his hands cupped to shout orders over the din of the engines. I couldn't help but giggle at how red his face was with the effort.

He looked up as Gonzo and I passed by. Even across a couple dozen yards, our eyes met and I could just about feel the heat of his frustrated rage.

Good!

I shouted so Gonzo could hear me. "I think it's working!"

"What?"

"I said it's *working*, Gonzo!"

He just replied with a thumbs-up.

As we came upon the third quarter, I saw that motorcycles still added to the double tail. Soon, the head would join the tail in a full circle of roaring bikes, and the siege would be underway.

That's when I noticed someone waving something big and blue at me from the outer sidewalk. Among a bunch more Star Troopers, Frannie swung my backpack back and forth, shouting at me.

I tapped Gonzo's shoulder and pointed. His head bobbed and we broke formation to glide over to where she stood. I hugged Gonzo once and then dismounted. Gonzo saluted and roared off to rejoin the others.

Frannie led me away from the roaring Circle so we could talk.

"Was this your idea?" asked Frannie as she handed me my backpack.

"I wish! Gonzo's a genius under that crass exterior!"

Frannie smiled. "What's next?"

"First things first," I said, rummaging around in my bag. I came up with the flask I'd brought for emergencies and unscrewed the lid.

"Is that such a good idea?" she said, pursing her lips into a disapproving little moue.

I tipped the flask back and my mouth filled with the burn of vodka. I let it run down my throat and I swallowed a few gulps before stopping. I took a deep breath of the thick Indiana summer air as warmth spread from my stomach out to my whole body.

"Why wouldn't it be a good idea, Fran?" I took another long drink to make a point.

She rolled her eyes. "Do you remember nothing from last night? You divulged the secrets of Big Con to a *horse*."

I shrugged. "That horse won't tell anyone."

Frannie made a Y with her arms and her eyes grew wide. "You mooned the beer garden at Heath's!"

I laughed. "I don't remember that, but it sounds like something I'd do."

"You threw up in front of Steak N' Shake, Skye!"

I took another shot of the vodka, my head starting to buzz. "Yeah, I remember that one. Sorry about that."

"I just wonder, with all that's going on right now, whether you'd be better off keeping your head straight?"

I shrugged. "Maybe. Maybe not. What if trolls show up? Who's gonna know?"

"Skye—"

"Me, that's who. And Minnie's out there somewhere, maybe she knows something important. Eh?"

Frannie shook her head. "If you say so. But just because you've got power, doesn't mean you should always use it."

I jerked a thumb at the Monument and the horde of enthralled humanity surrounding and covering it. "And who else is gonna stop them? You? Your power makes you extra vulnerable. I'd be crapping my panties right now if I were you."

She nodded. "Just about. But I know that booze doesn't help you with shadow, and I'm the only one here who can see more than meets the eye."

"Well see? There you go." I said, screwing the cap on the flask, now much lighter than it had been. I put it in my backpack and fished out my jeans and struggled into them. I fastened the button and zipped up and pulled the little skirt off and put it away. I kept the FFF warrior princess top and wore boots out of practicality.

"Now what are you doing?"

"I missed pockets. And can't put a scabbard on without a belt, either."

I found the belt and scabbard and belted on the Hilt. "If I'm a warrior princess, I should be armed and girded."

"Girded?"

"Sounded good. Whatever. I'm ready for anything now!"

At that moment, a fire truck roared into the circle, loud enough to be heard even over a hundred motorcycles. I saw it bounce up onto the sidewalk to dodge an abandoned police car, round the circle along with the bikers, then stop in front of Frannie and me, flashing lights giving me a headache.

A spotlight fixed us, and a small figure leaped out of the cab of the big ladder truck, heavy boots hitting the pavement with a thud.

I knew that silhouette.

"Annabelle!" I cried, and ran toward her.

She stood, hands on her hips, dressed in a full fire suit, everything covered in thick rubberized material except her head.

She still looked like an angel to me. Maybe more so with the dazzling light and apocalyptic scene behind her.

I threw my arms around her, but she stood stiff.

"So," The chill in Annabelle's voice froze my heart. "When you didn't answer my texts, at first I thought you might be working. So I waited until dinnertime to call you."

"Annabelle, I—"

She pushed me away. "Straight to voicemail. For hours. You'll have a laugh listening to all of my messages later. I'm sure you can convince everyone I'm your psycho ex-girlfriend."

Panic rose in my gut, and I had to take a couple shallow breaths before I could answer. "Ex-girlfriend? But sweetie!"

"Sweetie! Sweetie!" her tone was hurt and mocking at the same time. "I went on a fire call around then, and when we got back, it was all over the news, how there was this crazy zombie march that got out of control. Do you know why I grabbed this engine and came here? Homeland Security's orders! More are coming, Skye. I thought you might be in trouble, but I had no idea. I got here as fast as I could, and I find you here, booze on your breath, in the middle of a war zone."

"Yeah, I'm trying to stop Ernie—"

"Ernie, yeah Ernie. Always Ernie. Your dear husband."

"You know that's just a game! He's repulsive! And, and, he's evil!" I pointed at the zombie mass.

"And yet you're still his vampire bride, and you spend time with him like a friend!"

"Not anymore! I told him I wanted a divorce!"

She laughed. "Did you? And that didn't break his little heart?"

I shrugged. "Who cares? That's all just a game. He's gone bonkers, Belle, and I've got to make him stop before people get hurt."

She nodded. "Yeah, people are about to get hurt. Water cannons, tear gas, the works, to control this riot. Indianapolis is all over the news. CNN, the BBC, Al Jazeera, you name it."

"Will you help me?" I asked, in a small voice. I wondered if she even heard me over the noise.

She shook her head and bit her lip. The trail of a tear on her cheek shined with the flashing lights. "No. I'm sorry Skye, but no. I'm done. I can't do this anymore. You're a drunk, even when you're not saving the world from monsters. You go be a fantasy hero, waving your sword around, and I'll be the other kind of hero, out here on the ground."

"Please, Belle, please don't do this. I love you!"

"I loved you, Skye, I really did. But I can't do this anymore."

"You said us freaks have to stick together," I said, as though I were a lawyer, and I could *make* her stay with me.

She laughed. "Yeah, we do. But you have your own freakshow, Skye, and I'm not part of it. Sure, I tag along, just to be a part of your world, but what do we do *together*? What do you do to be a part of *my* world? Because I'll tell ya, *this* doesn't count!" She swept an arm around to take in the whole Circle.

Then she turned away and said, "I'm sorry, but I've got orders, and I've got work to do."

"Belle?"

She looked over her shoulder at me, eyes dangerous and hurt.

What I wanted to say was, "Please, don't leave me. I need you," but I didn't.

Instead, I said, "Don't let them touch you. You'll be assimilated."

"Yeah, Homeland Security figured that out, which is why I have the suit on. Go, Skye, just go, okay?"

The world blurred and my breath heaved and turned to sobs. I turned to get my backpack and run away. Frannie still stood there, forgotten. She held my backpack out to me and I took it, my whole body numb.

"Annabelle, she..." I didn't want to say it out loud, it might become real. "Oh Frannie, she—"

Frannie nodded. "Yeah, sorry, I heard. Let's go." She stuck out a hand and led me away from the fire truck as half a dozen more roared up.

The world dissolved into red and white lights, half-seen metal monsters, and swarms of people. I buried my face in Frannie's shoulder and bawled.

Whatever else happened tonight in this apocalyptic mess, I knew one thing for sure. *My* world had come to an end.

And I had nothing left to do but fight.

Chapter Nineteen

I don't know how long I bawled all over Frannie. Maybe a few minutes, maybe a lot longer. But at some point, the wracking pain collapsed into a horrible ache, and then that shrank to a frozen lump in the pit of my stomach, a cold bright point of hurt, remorse, and pure anger.

Over Frannie's shoulder, I watched a bulldozer push a police car out of the road. More fire trucks and panel vans trundled onto the Circle. Motorcycles scattered.

"I'm going in," I told Frannie, letting go of her.

"What? In where? No, Skye, let the authorities handle it."

I shook my head. "There's only one way it can be handled. I have to take away Ernie's mojo."

Frannie shook a finger in my face. "Skye, the sun doesn't rise and set on your command. We don't all just disappear when you close your eyes. You may be the hero of the movie of *your* life, but everyone else, they're stars in their own show. You're hurting, and I get that, I've been there. But this is no time to make rash decisions."

"They're still my decisions to make, and I'm getting sick of people telling me I'm rash or reckless or stupid. I'm the only one who can do it, and I have nothing left to lose."

Frannie slumped and rubbed her face with her hands. "There's always something else to lose, Skye. Always."

I straightened and wiped my eyes dry. We stared at each other for a long moment, sirens and engines and shouting all around us. *Time to go.* "Thanks for the shoulder, Frannie. Wish me luck?"

She shook her head. "No, I won't, because I don't think you should go. You're going to get hurt or killed, and you'll get others hurt or killed in the process."

"Fine. Sorry you feel that way." I turned and strode toward the circling motorcycles. *My cavalry.*

I took step after careful step across the bricks. The motorcycles only moved at a brisk walking pace, so they had plenty of time to see me. I got waves and salutes from the bikers as they drove past, making space for me to walk by dodging around me.

When I got to the other side, one motorcycle pulled up in front of me.

"Hey dumbass, you're going the wrong way," shouted Gonzo.

"You've slowed Ernie down, now it's my turn to stop him."

"How? You gonna make goo goo eyes at him? Maybe challenge him to arm-wrestling?"

I smiled and unfastened the chain around my neck and held the tiny bull-faced flask up for him to see. "I'm going to 'hold fast' like my ancestors."

"What, you're going to poison him? Or maybe a drinking contest?"

I grinned. "Now wouldn't that be heroic? Take a shot every time a zombie says 'brains'."

He shook his head. "Don't be stupid, Skye. There're thousands of brainless people between you and him. Even if you can probably beat him up with your bare hands, how are you going to get there?"

"Just watch me, I said," and I uncorked the tiny metal bottle.

A roaring began in my ears as the aroma of the liquor in the bottle. I'd sampled vodkas, schnapps of all flavors, scotch, bourbon and Irish whiskeys in my time. Nothing compared to this. Spicy like anise, potent like mint, strong like Everclear. Visible vapors streamed from the mouth of the flask, and I caught flashes of light, like fireflies in a summer bean field or the twinkle of stars through a heat haze.

It called to me. The aroma alone intensified my buzzing head, and the whisper of hundreds of voices jabbered among my thoughts. Many voices joined to create a single clear sentence, in the unmistakable tones of Bask, the Transit King. "Drink the last of me wonderbooze, and ye owe me, lassie."

I laughed. "To friends and love, eh Gonzo?"

He flipped me the bird. I raised the flask and tipped it back.

The essence of fairy flowed into me, skipping the part where my stomach ingested it. No, instead, I would swear the tiny sample filled my mouth and soaked right into my skin, and I thought of what Gonzo had said as a joke.

Poison! I'm dying! It's a trick, Bask's killing me!

And then the booze flowed over me, throughout me, *became* me.

My body was light as fog and as tough as titanium. The world around me misted over, but I saw clearer than ever. It was as though I turned inside out, and the core of me, some tiny part of my body and soul deep inside became all of me.

I saw through Gonzo and most of his motorcycle. The steel of his bike, like a skeleton, flared to become more real than real, even as Gonzo faded to a translucent wraith, studded with bits of harsh bright steel here and there.

I threw back my head and laughed long and loud, thrilling with the crackling power coursing through me. I cried, "Skyeing intensifying!"

As though from under water, Gonzo's voice floated to me. "What the crap, Skye? What did you do?" His eyes looked past me like the zombies had, but retained their intelligence as they darted around, searching for me.

"Ha ha, Gonzo, I am a real fairy now! I'm out of this world!" The booze felt like a beehive had taken up residence inside me. No, it was more like I'd split into thousands of bees that swarmed in a Skye-shaped space and became a hive entity. "Buzz, buzz, I am the queen bee, and my arms are full of drones!"

Something stabbed me along my waistline, something white-hot. I screamed and wriggled and pulled down my jeans and swatted at my lower back with the back of my hand. My hand burned and the smell of my own burned flesh conjured up a flash memory of touching a glowing electric stove element. I jerked my hand away with the same instinct that child had, and the clinking of metal on bricks at my feet made me jump back.

Oh, the nails! I'm vulnerable to iron now, like any other creature from the fairy world! This is amazing! I am Fairy Warrior Princess Skye, and I am going to kick some phony vampire ass!

I walked right past Gonzo, and on toward the crowd of dull-eyed humans that blocked my path.

And then, I passed through someone.

I almost threw up. Even though they were wispy, transparent beings to me, I still had a slimy sensation as my body occupied the same space as a small businesswoman. Her head occupied my chest cavity, and every bit of flesh on her, her bones, even each strand of hair pulled at my insides, just the tiniest of tugs. Like being filled with cobwebs.

I shuddered and did my best not to pass through anyone after that. I skirted the crowd and found a wall. I found I could climb it, making me wonder if I had Super Skye Strength or if my mass had dissipated to make me lighter for the climbing.

Whatever the reason, I scaled the wall and crawled along the sculpture where the zombie people could not go without great effort and thought.

I stood on a perch, my hand clinging to the elbow of a triple-sized concrete Civil War soldier as I leaned way out over the sea of dense packed humanity. The zombies crushed in, heaving to and fro as one, swaying to an unheard beat. The thrust of the crowd focused on the door to the interior of the monument. Ernie might not be able to call out over the motorcycle engines' roar to the whole crowd of his minions to give orders, but it seemed those close to him still did as he said. He called out, "One, two, three, *heave!*" over and over.

I could see no way to get to him without flying. *Well, why not, Skye? Right now you're a super-fairy, full of magical wonderbooze!*

I closed my eyes and imagined myself sprouting magnificent butterfly wings, as big as sails, fluttering over the crowd.

Two things happened at the same time. My feet left the ground, and my wings brushed the concrete soldier and knocked me off balance. I lost my grip on the sculpture and floated out in free space.

"Holy crap, I'm flying!"

My wings spread out to either side, flapping a lazy beat to keep me afloat. It reminded me of nothing so much as treading water, except up in the air.

I noticed something else. Everything appeared a bit larger than it had before. I smelled the crowd, and not just gamer funk, but individual scents, perfumes, food residues, the scents of leather and rubber and much more.

Even floating up here, I smelled Ernie's awful cologne. Despite that, I let out a whoop and fluttered down, closer and closer to him. I stared at him, knowing he could not see me. I let my wings take me right up to him.

He seemed ten feet tall to me. *Guess I shrank a bit when I got wings. Totally worth it!* Closer and closer until I got within reach. The spot at his neck revealed the ugly bear-face clasp. *Guess the shadow magic has less effect on me like this.* I saw now it had lost an "eye", only one gem glowed red at me out of its left eye socket.

I grabbed for it, and while my fingers met resistance, it was so much more solid than me. If I pulled, my fingers just slipped away, unable to hold on due to an unpleasant tingling like an electric shock and a strange sudden weakness.

I screamed in Ernie's face. "Give it up, you bastard!"

Just then, I heard bullhorns blare, and over Ernie's shoulder, I saw the edge of the crowd scatter like roaches with the light turned on. It looked like tear gas had parted the crowd. SWAT police in full riot gear and gas masks pushed their way in with tall clear plastic shields.

Ernie cursed, looking back toward these new sounds. "Come on, one more time!" he cried to the zombies. "One, two, three, PUSH!"

The crowd surged once more and the door crashed inward with the groaning of twisting metal and the triple pop of broken hinges. The zombies flooded into the stone building as one mass, a cattle call of thralls.

Ernie cheered and told his goons to hurry and carry him inside. Not knowing whether the gas might carry over to the fairy realm or what it could do to me, I followed right behind.

I had trouble with the doorway, and had to cling to Ernie with my wings folded. It took concentration to do even that, like grabbing onto whipped cream that turned to hard gelatin if I kept my mind focused.

Squishy and weird, I hated the sensation. Ernie brushed at his shoulders with his hands in an absent sort of way. I guessed he didn't notice my touch on a conscious level.

Probably for the best.

We moved inside, and Ernie had to get down from the goons. He instructed the big guys to keep a perimeter around him, which suited me fine. I let go of Ernie and willed my wings away. The room shrank and I resumed my usual Skye height, level with Ernie.

The horrible din outside was muffled inside the building, and I admit feeling relieved.

Ernie had more control over these hundred or so thralls since he could be more easily heard. "Okay, my loyal minions, on to the treasure!" He led them to a steel access door. He directed several to grab up replica Civil War carbines, complete with bayonets. He had several pry at the door with the bayonets, and they made slow progress.

Now I needed to make a move. People outside were being gassed and hurt.

The effect of the wonderbooze had passed its height and I knew my time was running out. I used the same sort of concentration to will myself to phase back into the mortal world.

I don't know how I'm getting out of here, but here goes nothing!

I grabbed at the amulet and Ernie screamed bloody murder. He slapped at me, and called for help.

Goons grabbed me and held my arms fast to my sides. I struggled but got nowhere.

"I don't know how you did that, but nice try, Skye." He looked me up and down. "I'm about to break through and then I'll be unstoppable."

"What kind of treasure could be worth all this, Ernie?"

He grinned. "Anything I want. A great power at my beck and call. Immortality, too, Skye. More power than even this bauble. It's just a piece of something far greater, and when it's reunited... Let's just say you'll be sorry you betrayed me."

"Ernie, what happened to you? You can be a real jerk a lot of the time, but I've never thought of you as *evil*."

"Evil? How melodramatic of you. Do you know what it's like to be looked over, spat on, never taken seriously?"

"Well, yeah, actually," I said, thinking of living on the streets of Chicago after my parents died.

"Screw you, Skye. You don't know. You're one of the beautiful people, one of the cute and fuzzy bunnies, and you make friends wherever you go. You get all your drinks for free; you get doors opened for you. You smile and guys fall over themselves to do whatever you want. This is *my* turn to get what you get naturally."

"You have no idea how wrong you are, Ernie. Did you know I've been homeless several times in my life? Did you know I'm an orphan? Have you ever *had* to depend on the kindness of others? Did you even stop to think that life might be as hard for everyone else as it is for you, in one way or another? Poor Ernie, no one likes him. As they say on the Internet, these are all just first world problems. You're a whiner who wants your own way, Ernie. You want friends? *Be* a friend. You want people to do things for you? Do things for other people. You want to be liked? Try being likeable for a change!" My voice rose to a shout without me realizing it.

Even though his goons held me in place, Ernie took a step back. He turned his head, distracted for a moment as the doorway began to give to the zombies' prying and pulling. Even from across the room, I could see their fingers had turned red, bleeding with the effort of pulling at the steel door.

"Shut up, Skye. Just shut up. Game's almost over, and I'm going to win."

My head swam, and I knew my magical booze would wear off soon. "Well, I didn't stop you, but you're not taking me down with you, Ernie. Can't say I didn't try."

I concentrated and phased into the fairy realm once more, my arms and body passing through the big guys like slimy spider webs trailing over and through my diaphanous body.

Ugh, nasty! I'd never get used to that!

I took a step away from them. I laughed as Ernie's head whipped this way and that, looking for me.

Neat trick, wish I could always do it!

He let out a gurgly frustrated noise, and then ordered his goons to make a path for him to the door. He strode through the parted crowd to join the zombies who pried at the door, urging them on. Those shredded fingers worked, painting the sharp edge of the steel door a vivid red with their blood.

Maybe I'd better see what's ahead. I took advantage of the cleared path to walk right up to the door and took a deep breath to walk right *through* it.

If I had walked into a vertical greasy spoon grill, it would have hurt less. I smelled burning Skye. I allowed myself to fall to the floor rather than touch the wall again to push off.

Holy crap! Who makes a door out of solid iron?

My screams went unheard, and I had to scramble through the wet tissue paper of zombie bodies to get out of the way; something in the door snapped and it swung open.

A gust of dry, earthen air poured into the room, a scent I found familiar but couldn't place right away. Stairs descended into inky darkness.

Ernie cheered and ran on ahead first, followed by his goons and a slow procession of his other thralls nearby. Bloody-handed zombies carried their carbines like soldiers, trotting behind, down the stairs.

In desperation, I imagined myself becoming Tinker Bell, since only a tiny pixie could get around this crowd without wading through their disgusting innards out of phase.

To my delight, the room became large, then huge, then ginormous. I flitted up to the ceiling. A soft glow emanated from my body, showing a limited space around me. I used that to keep from hitting the ceiling or passing through the skull of one of the enslaved people below.

The stairs wound down and down, past concrete walls, down to where the walls turned to brick like I'd seen in the catacombs.

The catacombs! Is this part of that? Holy crap, maybe Ernie's treasure is guarded by the Chained Lord himself!

The stairs widened, the air grew chill, and the dark even more intense, almost tangible. Several of the enslaved people tripped and fell into others, falling like human dominoes.

Not one of them cried out in pain, but instead got up and resumed their plodding.

Ernie called back in an irritated tone, telling the zombies to use their phones' lights to see.

Several dozen lights sprang to life, but the gloom of the deep stairwell sucked at their brilliance, dulling them to mere glowing rectangles in the dark.

Still, it was enough to keep more from tripping. I urged my hummingbird wings on, feeling the burn in my shoulder blades as they sped me forward and down, passing above the heads of these poor lost souls.

I reached the bottom only seconds after Ernie and his brainless lieutenants, and he gaped as the phones' flashlights failed to pierce the blackness of the room at the bottom.

A voice boomed in the dark, and two red slits opened, higher than Ernie's head, but close enough to cause him to stumble backward.

"I've been waiting for you, mortal."

Chapter Twenty

Ernie stammered and sputtered, unable to get out any clear words.

I'd love to say something smug here, that I felt no pity for Ernie or that I'd been ready for this, having met the Chained Lord before and had drinks with him.

I'd be lying. All I knew was that those eyes burned in the dark, and his chains glowed a dim silver light that I could only see if I looked at something else.

"Welcome back, fairykin. I see you've brought a friend!" That voice, more terrible than the hundred motorcycles of my cavalry far above our heads, shook my tiny pixie body and blew me back a foot or two.

Ernie replied, "I am no fairy. I seek the treasure. I've brought the amulet. I've mastered it in ways no mortal has before, not even the one who fell in the asylum where I found it. I come for the rest. And I've brought an army. At my command, they'll pull you apart, you big thing in the dark."

The Chained Lord pulled at his chains and backed up a step. "Let's be polite now, shall we?" He snapped his fingers and I *saw* a shock wave of energy ripple out through the room like a rock dropped in a still pond.

The energies had no effect I could see on the dozens of zombies that flooded the room, not even Ernie's looming guards.

When the blast hit me, however, I inflated and fell and hit the brick floor with a heavy thump of my full human-Skye form, and my breath left me for a minute. I kicked at zombies who strayed too close to me as I struggled from prone to a crouch.

The room rumbled with the deep engine rumble of the Chained Lord's laugh.

"Don't..." I fought for breath. "Don't hurt them, please?"

"Hmm, they intend me harm. I am bound. What choice do I have, scion of MacLeod?"

"What's he talking about, Skye?"

"If you sic these poor gamers and bikers on that ancient troll king, they're going to die."

I couldn't see Ernie's face in the dark. "Or he's bluffing. Chained up down here, he's either grown weak or the chains have him too restrained to fight back."

"If I free you, your majesty, will you promise you won't hurt Ernie's slaves?"

More engine rumbling mirth made the walls tremble. "You have a deal, fairykin."

I drew the Fairy Hilt, and though the wonderbooze buzz was faint, the vodka I'd chugged before Annabelle... before then, was not. The ancestral intangible magic fairy blade of my clan burned with a cold, terrible light. In this place, perhaps between worlds somehow, even Ernie and the zombies turned to look at me as I stepped to the wall and examined where the chain was bolted to the wall. *No way do I want to get close to that giant troll.*

Ernie called an order to his zombies, but not fast enough... I swung the Fairy Hilt, and its glowing blade passed through the chain.

Since I felt no impact, I thought for half a second that it hadn't helped. Then I saw that I'd cut in two the silvery runes that had encased the chains, the magic that held him here. Each half of the glowing spell sparked and went dark, spreading backward from my sword's touch.

Tiny sparks sprayed my skin. Some instinct pushed me a step back from this reaction. *It's kind of like a great big sparkler.*

Ernie yelled for the zombies to attack and kill the great troll. The Chained Lord pulled his wrists together, and when the sparkler effect reached the one manacle, it spread to the other, and on through the other chain to the wall.

The great troll heaved one way and the chain pulled apart and fell limp on the ground. He heaved the other and the bolts pulled from the stone wall and he was free.

The Chained Lord roared and stretched, and I had to cover my ears in pain. He pressed his hands to the ceiling, shoving at the brickwork, and chunks of masonry rained down on him, bouncing off his body.

The zombies clustered around him, clawed at his stony flesh and climbed his legs.

He brushed them from him without much effort.

He kept his word; they seemed unharmed, though more piled on right away.

No damage showed on him, either.

Ernie shrieked, "I demand my treasure! It told me I'd awaken the power that it came from!"

The Chained Lord's laugh fell deeper than human hearing, but I felt my own chest resonate with the low frequency. Its power was so potent that my breath came into my chest and out again with each boom.

"And you have gotten it! The amulet is my creation, stolen from me by shadow creatures even as I was betrayed and locked here."

Ernie held the amulet up before him like a shield to ward off the monstrous troll king. "Then that must mean you are mine to command!"

I had to admit, Ernie put on a good front, but I heard the quiver in his voice.

The Chained Lord thrust his hand at Ernie and pinned the gawky vampire role-player to the wall, stone thumb and forefinger on either side of his chest. Ernie screamed and though I felt no warmth for him, there was no way I'd stand by and watch him die.

"I hope I don't have to remind you of your promise, your majesty," I said, taking a step closer with my bright fairy blade.

He turned his head to regard me. "Indeed, I keep my promise. None of this maggot's thralls will be harmed by my volition. Nothing was said about this arrogant fool's well being. I will take the amulet from him and then I shall bite his head from his shoulders to make a point."

Typical fairy lawyer crap. Nothing was said about my well being, either!

Ernie gasped and squeaked. He said, "Help me, Skye!"

"How about this, if he gives up the amulet, you won't harm either Ernie or me?"

The Chained Lord growled. "That does not benefit me. My plan leaves me unfettered. And I am so weary of bonds, fairykin."

"Oh but it does. Because if you don't agree, I'm going to see what this magic sword does to you."

The Chained Lord squinted at me in the light of the Fairy Hilt. "Fine. You have a bargain, but put away the sword and he has to give up the amulet immediately!"

A few loose bricks fell from the ceiling as the troll king shouted at me.

I nodded and sheathed the Fairy Hilt.

"Ernie!" My voice made his head snap up, and we locked eyes. "Give it up."

He said, "But Skye—"

"End this. NOW!" I said, cupping my hands in front of me.

Understanding dawned in his eyes and he tossed the amulet underhand toward me. I caught it.

Every zombie in the room slumped to the floor at the same time.

The Chained Lord roared, and more bricks rained down. One glanced off my left shoulder and my arm went numb.

"Skye!" The tiny voice of Minnie came to me from the doorway to the hall, cracked open a few inches. Red torchlight spilled in. "Run, you idiot, follow me!"

I shoved the amulet in my pocket and followed Minnie's voice and shoved the door open wide. The roar of the Chained Lord came to me and he struggled into the tunnel, crawling on all fours behind us.

Too late to grab a torch without getting within troll-grasping range, I dashed into the dark after Minnie.

I could see her in the dark, even without light. She bounded down the hall with a strange motion, as though each small step took her further than my strides. I tripped and fell once or twice, knees battered on the gravel-strewn dirt floor. I gave thanks that I'd thought to change into jeans instead of that silly little costume skirt, or I'd have left skin and blood behind.

I willed myself to have Minnie's magical speed, and I kept pace with her, sort of stitching space together so that each step counted for more. The magic of the wonderbooze no longer burned fierce in my belly, but guttered like the stub of a candle.

Soon, that last bit of power fizzled and I felt fatigue wash over me, and I lost the nifty long stride ability. Minnie gained on me.

Even still, the giant troll fell behind, hampered by the smaller passageways.

Not far enough behind for comfort! I wish I could see better!

Then a funny thing happened. Despite the wonderbooze wearing off, my wish fulfilled, and my sight showed sketchy outlines of walls, and when I held up my hand, it seemed like my skin glowed with some sort of dim, pale light.

The pounding of enormous feet startled me out of my momentary wonder. *No time to think about it now!*

Minnie had to stop for me a couple of times. "Hurry it up, Skye! You've really screwed the pooch this time!"

"*Et tu*, Minnie?"

"I got your back, sis, always. But you freed the ancient troll. Think maybe they chained him up for a reason?"

"He'd have killed those poor people," I said, panting as we rounded a corner.

"So now he's gonna kill us instead, gotcha."

We encountered Brick and Limestone, a half dozen other trolls lined up behind them.

I found one of my hands in the pocket that contained the amulet. The thought came to me that I could, with a touch, make these other trolls do my bidding just as Ernie had controlled people at Big Con and on the streets of Indy. I imagined them holding the hallway behind us to slow the Chained Lord down so we could escape.

I shook off those thoughts.

Instead, I drew my sword. The light of the Fairy Hilt's blade glinted in their narrowed eyes. Also, their king's frustrated bellow and sounds of him crashing through the tunnel came echoing down the hallway at our heels. They fled without a word. I picked up a torch one of them dropped in his panic. The strange night vision vanished in this more normal light. I decided that I preferred the fire's light.

"I can't keep this up, Minniekins!"

"Follow me!" she said, dashing down a smaller hallway. Far too small for the Chained Lord to follow, and small enough that I had to stoop and slow down.

Minnie turned down another, and a terrible zoo odor assaulted my sense of smell.

"We're now entering Goblin country," she said. "Mind your manners and we may just get out alive, Skye."

"Oh, 'gobbos'," I said.

"Goblin etiquette lesson number one: The trolls call them 'gobbos'. It's a sort of racial slur. Don't use that word."

"Got it!"

A troop of gnarled little creatures detached themselves from the walls and blocked out path. They seemed to be made of mud and roots and bits of brick and rock. They stood maybe twice Minnie's height, maybe waist high on me, and three times her girth. When they spoke, all I could think of was large talking toads.

"Awright! Hoot goes? Whassa noise? World coming to an end, is it?" said the leader, who carried a steak knife as a small sword.

"The Chained Lord has escaped! We are fleeing him, can you help us?" said Minnie.

"Hur hur hur. He's stuck, tha one. Hunnerds of yars. Yer fibbing an' we don't hold wit that."

Booming thunder, accompanied by the roar of the Chained Lord's fury echoed down the hall at our backs.

The goblins' watery eyes doubled in size and they backed up, out of the ring of flickering light of my torch.

"Wait, come back, please!" I said, stepping up to try to catch up with them.

"We don' hafta be faster than His Monstrousness, we jes hafta be faster than you!"

"Show us the way out, and I'll... well, I promise to tell you the story."

"Wha story?"

"The story of how the Chained Lord became unchained."

"Lady, we don' wanna know."

"Look, what if I told you *I* freed him?"

"I'd say yer a terrible liar or yer dumber than a bag of bricks."

I reached. "What if I told you that he's after me in particular? And I've just led him to your warrens? And the longer I stay here, the harder he's going to pursue us?"

The craggy little goblins conferred in a whisper.

As they talked among themselves, I added, "Show us out, and I promise to make a lot of noise outside to draw him out."

They grunted and waved me to follow.

Minnie hopped onto my shoulder and hung on as I hunched my way down even smaller passages, which now sloped upward.

The howls of the ancient troll receded behind us, and the quiet of the dirt-and-stone walls of the tunnel muffled even our own footsteps. At one point, all sounds of pursuit stopped.

Some twists and turns forced me to crawl and climb through passages not much taller than the goblins. My hands became caked in clay, and my jeans soaked through with the damp earth. *I'm going to look like a giant goblin before we reach the surface, aren't I?*

The tunnel widened into a room that had many other tunnels splitting off at other angles. The room had one flat concrete wall, with a metal door with a wheel in the center that reminded me of a submarine. It said "SEWER IDPW" in rusty raised letters.

The steak-knife-wielding goblin pointed his weapon at the closed portal. "Hur, if you kin get past that, yer free. Better hope yah can hold yer nose an' run fast."

Chapter Twenty-One

After the goblins vanished down a different tunnel, Minnie and I stood alone in the connecting chamber, staring at the iron door.

"What are you waiting for, biggun?" she said.

I reached for the wheel, and then stopped. Various angry burns all over my body suggested that turning that iron wheel might be a nasty, white-hot experience. "Well. That wonderbooze, it made me a full fairy for awhile. I'm kinda scared of it, Minniekins."

She clucked her tongue, "Well, it won't hurt me a lot, but it's too big for me to turn. Do you still feel like a fairy?"

I closed my eyes and thought about it. No bees buzzing in my body, no electrical current running through me. I tried to grow wings. Nothing. I willed myself to fly.

The floor fell away from me, and below me I heard a woman say, "Holy crap!"

The voice sounded just like mine. I looked down to see my body standing there. *So that's what the back of my head looks like!*

I heard myself laugh, and Minnie said, "Skye? What's going on?"

Cool, this must be what it's like to be Frannie!

I floated around the room, but as soon as I moved more than a few feet from my body, a tugging like a leash held me back. A thick silver rope or cable connected me to my body.

So, not exactly like Frannie.

"Skye. What are you doing, just standing there? Hello? Hello?"

Even though the new discovery filled me with a giddy glee, I returned to my body to answer Minnie. Which turned out to be a little like waking up from a dream where I've fallen from a short height. I jumped, and took a deep breath. My heart pounded in my chest.

Minnie climbed up me to look me in the eye and slap me on the cheek with her tiny hand. "Biggun, what's wrong?"

"Minnie, I uh, picked up that thing Ernie had."

"You *picked up* the evil artifact he used to make a zombie army?"

I nodded. "Yeah. He threw it to me as part of the deal with the Chained Lord."

"The Chained Lord wanted you to have it?"

I ached to learn what other things I could do with the amulet. "Noooo... He wants it for himself, bad. I, uh, well—"

"Skye! Spit it out! You're killing me here!"

I smiled. "Well, what can I say? I tricked him."

She smacked her forehead with the palm of her hand. "Oh no."

"Oh yes! It was the only way to save Ernie and free those poor people, Minnie. And I think it'd be a bad idea if Mr. Rocky Pants gets a hold of the amulet."

"Why?"

"He said it's something he made, right before being thrown in chains in that dungeon, hundreds of years ago. If Ernie, who has no powers, can do what he did, just imagine what a powerful guy who doesn't need an owner's manual could do with it?"

"Maybe. But what's the idea of working with shadow magic anyway? He'd be out of his element, crossing two worlds to work those energies." She frowned.

I thought a minute and said, "Fairy and shadow don't cross over much?"

She laughed. "Try never. I can't say they're opposites, but you and I are the closest they come."

"Huh?"

"Well, I split off you after a shadow demon possessed you, right? But somehow your fairy heritage made that work different. Frannie's soul lives out in shadow. I think you'd be more like her if you'd started off without that background."

"I just had an out of body experience, Minnie, thanks to the amulet. It's answered my desires twice now."

"Twice?"

"Yeah, back before we saw the other trolls, I wanted to see in the dark, and voila! I could, sort of."

"So I'd say you're pretty safe to touch the iron, since fairy and shadow never cross."

I shrugged and she bobbed up and down. "Guess I can test it out."

She hopped down and stood nearby while I approached the big iron wheel. I reached out my hand and extended just my pinky finger. *No sense getting burns on an important finger.*

I closed the distance, afraid as much of smelling my own flesh burn as the burn itself. I touched it. I jerked back at the first sensation. Cold, raspy, and just a touch of something like electricity tickled the nerves of my pinky finger.

I sighed relief and grabbed the wheel with both hands. The tingling intensified, but below a painful threshold. I heaved, but the wheel didn't budge.

"Well?"

"I feel something, but no Skye frying this time. Can't move it, I'm not strong enough."

"Well we can't go back," she said.

"Yeah, yeah, I know. Hang on." I had an idea. I closed my eyes and reached into that place where I'd gotten the night vision and the out of body experience. I drew on the amulet's power and imagined myself strong like Xena or Buffy. I pictured the old Incredible Hulk TV show, myself as Bill Bixby swelling into Lou Ferigno.

I shoved at the wheel. "You wouldn't. Like me. When. I'm. ANGRY!" I was rewarded with a rusty squeal of protest as the wheel turned and hidden bolts slid back. I pulled the hatch open with a whoop of joy, cold fire burning all along my arms and back. Almost an anti-fire, dark flames licked along my skin. It felt good in an uneasy way.

Minnie hooted and hopped through the portal.

I took a breath, blew it out, and the cold fire extinguished all at once.

A girl could get used to this kind of power. Then I remembered Ernie ranting about power in the dealer hall. Just the memory of the crazy look in his eyes made me shiver. I resolved to keep tabs on thoughts like that.

I followed Minnie through the portal and found myself in a long concrete cylinder, a trickle of sludgy water all along the bottom. We stood to one side, on the curve of the pipe.

Shouts came from the direction we'd come.

I pulled the rusty iron hatch shut and turned the wheel. I left the superpowers to the Hulk and just used my ordinary Skye strength to crank it shut. The iron still tickled like a current passing through my hands, but it did me no harm.

We scrabbled our way along the tunnel, keeping clear of the sewage at the bottom. Walking on the curved incline made movement slow and awkward while carrying my torch, but soon, I caught sight of a ladder up ahead.

Iron again. I had Minnie climb on my back. She clung to my shoulders as I grabbed the lowest rung and pulled myself up. More electricity, bearable and ticklish at worst. Same when I pushed up the manhole cover at the top. I peeked out and when no giant troll came stomping my way, I pushed the heavy lid aside and climbed out into the middle of a street. East New York Street, the sign said. Other than some parked cars and lights in a couple of houses nearby, Minnie and I had the street to ourselves.

Minnie laughed. "Wouldn't it have been funny if we'd escaped a ten ton pissed-off troll only to get hit by a car climbing out of the sewer?"

"No, not so funny," I said, but I smiled at her.

I replaced the metal manhole cover with a terrible clang and managed not to lose any fingers doing it. When I finished, I found Minnie staring off behind me, her face lit with odd flashes of different colored light.

She pointed.

I turned around to see the skyline of downtown, maybe a half mile away now. Helicopters hovered low here and there, spotlights focused on something unseen. Orange light flickered off some of the buildings, and a crack-BOOM echoed down the canyons of tall buildings like thunder. A familiar roar, far off, reached my ears.

Just then, headlights rounded the corner and came straight at us. Minnie and I got out of the street, and a city bus pulled up and stopped right in front of us.

The door opened, revealing the driver to be Bask, the Transit King. "Get in, ye great galloping idiot," he said, his face full of brewing storms.

"Uh, thanks, I can walk back," I said.

He shook his head. "T'wasn't a request, lass. Get on me bus. Now."

I looked at Minnie and she nodded and slid down me and disappeared into the night, back toward the mass chaos I'd helped create.

The bus's horn sounded twice and I cursed and climbed the stair and sat in one of the front seats so I could see Bask as he drove.

The doors shut with an ominous hiss, and the IndyGo bus lurched forward.

I started to speak, "Bask—"

"Hand it o'er, lass. Do it now."

"What?"

"Ye know what I mean. The shadow mojo, the artifact."

"How do you know—"

"Shut it. There's a great rampagin' troll breaking yer city righ' now, and ye've got the one thing it wants more than the freedom ye gave it, ye dumbass."

"I *had* to! He'd have killed—"

"An' I said shut it and hand it o'er, lass."

A chill gripped my heart at the thought of parting with the amulet. "I *need* it to take on the Chained Lord, Bask!"

"I won't ask again. Skye MacLeod, I claim my favor for drinkin' me wonderbooze. Anythin' I want, ye ken? And I want that trinket. Ye've made enough mess; ye've played with fire long enough, girl. Let a grownup fix yer mess."

"No." The word tumbled out of my mouth without any conscious thought attached to it.

His head snapped around, his eyes locked mine with his fierce, bright, dangerous eyes, under bushy brows. "I did nae hear ye right. The righ' answer is 'here ye go, kindly Transit King, this is me keepin' my end of a promise between us'. Now say again?"

I shook my head. "No. Sorry. I need it. I have to do this."

"If ye refuse, ye will be a liar, an oathbreaker in my eyes, lass. We'll be done, an' no fairy folk who hear your name will trust yer word e'er again. Tha's worse than ye ken. Last time. Give me the shadow-thing, Skye."

I pulled the cord. The STOP REQUESTED sign lit with a ding. I stood up, holding onto an overhead rail. "I'm getting off here, driver."

"Oathbreaker!" hissed the Transit King, and he pulled the bus to the curb. His face lit up as a helicopter's spotlight played on the bus, through the windshield. I expected rage or disgust, but instead his eyes looked on me with deep sadness.

"Off with ye, then," he said, opening the bus's door. Fear replaced sadness in those eyes. "Skye, next time we meet, someone'll die."

"Is that a threat?" I said, a cold pit growing in my stomach.

"Nae, lass," he said in hushed tones. "'Tis prophecy, it came to me in a flash. Shadow borders the land o' the dead. The trinket taps into tha', it calls out to be fed by death. 'Ware our next meeting. An' don't get hit by a bus!"

My heart filled with lead and tears welled in my eyes and his face blurred through them as I passed him.

I stepped off the bus and left the funny little gnome to drive his bus away.

Once again, I saw fire and flashing emergency lights through my tears. I blinked them away as best I could, and saw I'd been dropped off near the Circle, even though the bus had been traveling away from downtown when it picked me up. On a one-way street.

Dread grew within me, and my legs rebelled against the direction I walked. Each step took me closer to the Circle, and deep down I knew what I'd find, and I knew I was at least partly to blame. *If only I'd stopped Ernie sooner! If only I hadn't freed the Chained Lord!*

"If only you'd listened to your boss," came a voice from the shadows. I whirled to see a familiar figure step out into a pool of streetlight.

Rebecca Burton, my paranormal investigator employer, approached me. *Guess now's not a good time to ask for a raise.*

Chapter Twenty-Two

She still wore her trademark hat, her red hair and casual business suit somehow perfect despite the chaos going on around us.

"Rebecca! How did you?"

Her expression unreadable, my boss said, "Sorry, Skye, no time for pleasantries. Too much is going on. But you know that."

"It's hard to miss," I said, glancing at the flame-lit Monument a block away.

"You had one job, Skye. Observe, then report back to me. That's all."

Another lecture? Oh no. I've had enough of that already. "You weren't there, and you have no idea what I've been through!"

Her smile contained no humor. "I know more than you think. You've had many choices, and you made every one wrong. Now you're about to make another bad choice, and maybe you'll get killed, or maybe more people will die because of what you choose."

She put out a hand, palm up, and before I could reply, she said, "Hand it over."

"Hand what over?"

"Don't insult me, Skye. The artifact. The amulet. It's too much for you to handle. Even if you win the day, it'll change you. Like it did Ernie."

"Maybe it's the wrong choice, but it's mine to make. I am not giving it up. Not until I've fixed one of my mistakes. The big one that I guess is stomping around downtown as we talk."

She nodded and put away her hand. "Your choice. But know this. Ernie's been shot."

Another chill passed through me. "He has?"

Rebecca nodded. "Homeland Security identified him as the cause of the riots, and despite my best efforts, they deployed a sniper to take him out when he reappeared from the Monument."

Tricky Skye can control fairies with promises, but not people. Not without this nasty little artifact, anyway. "Oh no. Is he dead?"

Rebecca shrugged. "I don't know. Everyone fell to the ground before he emerged, and so they had a clear shot and they took it. I think he was alive when the SWAT team extracted him. Then the Chained Lord dug his way out of the Monument. Made a hole you could drive an ambulance through. Damnedest thing though, he smashed masonry, knocked cars and soldiers out of his way, but walked almost daintily through the unconscious bodies. Like an elephant, afraid to step on mice."

"I did that. He's bound by a fairy promise not to hurt Ernie's thralls."

Rebecca pursed her lips. "Hmm. Technically, they're not his thralls anymore."

I shrugged. "Then he held to the spirit of the agreement, not the letter."

Rebecca nodded. "Go see what you've done. You made your choice, and I'm making mine. I wish you well, Skye, and I hope you get your head together before it's too late. But I'm letting you go. I can't have someone so reckless working for me."

Fired, twice in one day. At least it's too late to disappoint Annabelle.

As upset as I'd been the first time I'd been fired today, I took it well. No tears, no arguing, I just swallowed it. "Yeah, okay. Sorry I let you down, Rebecca."

She moved to touch my shoulder with her hand, but I backed up a step. I don't know why, but some gut instinct said that if she touched me, I'd give up the amulet. "Thanks, but I'm good."

Rebecca frowned and took a step back. "Try not to do anything stupid, Skye. You're carrying the shadow equivalent of a nuclear weapon in your pocket; you're smarting from rejection and defeat. Remember your clan's creed."

With a touch to the brim of her hat, and without another word, she turned and walked away, down an alleyway.

Rather than hot remorse, cool relief flooded through me. I balled up my fists, took a breath, and sprinted the remaining block to the Circle.

Motorcycles lay on their sides everywhere, like giant metal bugs killed by insecticide. Instead of thousands of mindless zombies, I found dozens of ambulances, people lying on gurneys and stretchers and even on blankets laid out on the bricks. Several cars had been smashed in by giant troll feet, others had been turned on their sides or upside down, gasoline fires being fought by the engines present. I saw a diminutive firefighter at the front, guiding a hose with two other bigger firefighters. I didn't know for certain it was Annabelle, but my heart still ached at the sight.

I heard a man yell, "There she is!"

The L.T. and Ham ran up to me. I'd only just met them, but the ice in my heart melted just a bit at the sight of them standing.

"Dumb bitch!" said the L.T. as he grabbed me into a hug.

"We thought you were dead," added Ham. Ash coated his face and dusted his hair, aging him twenty years.

I let the L.T. hug me. *Guess the perv has a heart under all that show.*

He let go and Ham exchanged a look with him.

"Guys, I have to go after that troll. What did you see when it broke out of the Monument?"

"A friggin' troll, just like you said!" said the L.T.

"Huh. Guess he's too big to disguise with a glamour."

"Yeah, and it was weird. All these football players, or big fans wearing their colors, came rushing out after the troll."

I nodded. "More trolls."

"Figures. Because those guys were dicks. They got in the way of our motorcycles. Bikes hit these guys, even, and just got knocked over."

Ham said, "Before you go after them, I have to show you something." I'd never seen him not smiling before.

I followed them through motorcycles, around ambulances, to a gurney on a curb. Gonzo lay on it, eyes staring up, chest heaving. His shirt dark with blood, he pulled an oxygen mask from his face for a moment and said, "Dammit, Skye."

"Glad to see you too, Gonz."

He coughed and winced and his eyes focused on me. "I don't know how much of this was you, but I gotta tell you something."

I waited for yet another lecture.

"You're a good kid, but you're an amateur drunk. Get your shit together, Skye."

His words sank in and spoke to me in ways the Transit King and Rebecca hadn't. Some things clicked into place inside me, and I said, "I know, Gonz. I know what I have to do now. Thanks. Are you going to be okay?"

He put the mask back on to take a deep breath before answering, "Takes more than a rampaging elephant and a football team to get ole Uncle Gonzo down. Get out of here, do what you gotta."

A paramedic shooed us away and made Gonzo lie still. I walked a few steps away with Ham and the L.T.

"Is he going to be okay, guys?"

They exchanged another glance and Ham said, "They don't know. He got thrown off his bike and into a car. He's got a concussion, some broken bones, and he's lost a lot of blood. If it was just him, I'd say yeah, but look around you. Too many injured."

I bit my lip and hugged each of them. Ham smelled like peppermint, and he squeezed me like an old friend.

"I gotta go, guys," I said. My eyes stung, and I wiped away the beginnings of more tears.

"Go," said Ham, "We'll take care of Gonzo."

The L.T. grabbed my shoulder and said to him, "I'm with her. That cool, dude?"

Ham nodded. The L.T. looked at me, and I nodded.

We wove our way among the wreckage. *At least he won't be hard to find.* "I think I know where he's headed."

"Big Con?"

"Yep."

The L.T. had many friends among the bikers who still hung out. Several ran up to him and he explained we were going after the troll. More joined up. Soon, I had a couple dozen biker guys and gals trailing in my wake. We followed the path of destruction. Pavement cracked like eggshells in places from the Chained Lord's feet most of the way. More overturned cars, too. Stoplights and power lines hung from poles. Broken glass and other debris crunched under all our feet as we marched along. I thanked myself for putting on boots earlier.

We didn't talk much. The damage, and the thought of the strength necessary to create it, had us all on high alert, eyes and ears open, mouths shut. It seemed an unnatural state for the L.T., but with real danger up ahead, I suppose his military training had kicked in. It helped my mood, just a little, having someone with actual training and maybe combat experience along.

We caught up with Phil and several other Star Troopers along the way to the convention center. I admit I cried again when I found Phil alive. I told him my plan, and he said, "You're crazy, Skye. I've seen you through this far, though, and I don't have anything better. Let's go."

So, my ragtag army grew.

A group of my vampire gaming community came along for the ride too. You'd think after the brawl last year and the giant troll that'd knocked over and crushed cars all along his path down the street, that they'd just run away. But maybe it was surviving last year's insanity that made them crazy enough to follow me once again.

I kept telling myself, I didn't ask a single one of them to follow. I made a point of not touching the amulet, though it called out to me from inside my pants pocket. It wanted to be used, and a hunger for that power ate at me.

Then I'd picture Ernie at the center of all those zombies, and I'd push back, shoving those thoughts away. *That's not who I am.*

The convention center loomed ahead, glass doors caved in, metal frames twisted and broken.

The troll I nicknamed Obsidian stood at the door with a dozen other trolls of various shapes and sizes. My army of a hundred bikers and gamers seemed fragile all of a sudden, flesh against stone.

I stood at the front and said in as commanding a tone as I could manage, "Stand aside, doorman. I'm here to challenge your King."

Obsidian growled. "This is the Chained Lord's time, fairykin. Not only is he our King, he is yours too. All will fall before him as the prophesy foretold."

"Prophesy?"

"Ancient troll lore says that one day a mortal would free the Chained Lord and he would walk free and all would bow to his magnificence."

I smirked. "I bet he made that up himself to tell as a bedtime story. He's pretty ancient. Who's going to say otherwise?"

Obsidian glared at me. "Go away, mortal, and take your fleshbag followers with you."

"I think if you check your boss's appointment book, you'll find me penciled in for a showdown. You see, I've got something he wants." I took out the amulet to show him. A chill calm flooded through me as I touched the metal. The trolls' threat seemed laughable. All I had to do was touch one of them and they'd follow me and do anything I said.

And trust me, I *wanted* to touch them and make them mine, I really did. I *ached* for it. It took everything in me to put the amulet away after giving him a peek.

Obsidian ground his teeth and shouted to the other trolls, "Grab the fairykin! Take that thing from her!" He reached out a hand and grabbed my arm.

I grabbed the Fairy Hilt and pulled it from its scabbard. The blade flamed to life, and I lopped off Obsidian's arm at the elbow. The stump glowed like molten lava. The shiny stone fingers on my arm released and the arm hit the pavement and shattered. I could have taken his head off instead, but I wasn't done talking to him. He screamed, and the other trolls hesitated.

"I'd like to see you try. Go, and tell him I'm coming, doorman."

Obsidian waved his stump around, his mouth worked but no words came out, and his eyes darted around in panic.

The other trolls broke and ran into the convention center. I leveled the tip of the MacLeod ancestral blade at Obsidian's chest, and he turned and followed the others.

Chapter Twenty-Three

"Uh, Skye, what just happened?" The L.T.'s voice held a husky edge that told me I'd seen things they hadn't.

I turned around to survey the brave people who'd come to fight with me. My followers wielded crowbars, motorcycle locks, knives, baseball bats, tire tools and boards with nails in them. The nails, the tire tools and crowbars might hurt them, if they counted as iron. Maybe a dozen had firearms of one kind or another, a couple of shotguns and a bunch of pistols. I had no idea if those would harm a troll. Some wore plastic Star Trooper armor, others wore leathers, some carried prop shields, but most had no protection at all.

If I was leading them into a fight, they needed to know more about what they'd be up against.

I spoke to the whole group. "Look, I need to tell you something crazy, okay? You all saw the big troll back there? Well these guys at the door, they looked like trolls to me too, just on a smaller scale. What did you see?"

A biker girl spoke up. "I saw a bunch of guys in football jerseys. Most of them pretty big. No weapons."

The L.T. chimed in. "And that one dude just walked up and got in your face and you showed him a badge or something. When he grabbed you, you whipped out that handle or whatever from your holster and then… well, I'm not sure how, but his arm fell off and broke into pieces on the ground. Then they all ran away."

Murmurs of agreement rippled throughout the crowd.

The biker girl called out, "Bullshit. This is crazy. She's crazy."

I hadn't noticed her among the crowd before, but Raven spoke up. "I came to help. Skye's the real deal. I saw some things last year that made no sense, and I never bought that they were hallucinations from spiked punch. Skye led a bunch of us in a battle against a bunch of wolf monsters, and we won. Well except that one guy, Stuart."

I winced. "That was my fault. And if anyone wants to bug out now, I don't blame you. I don't want to be here either, but someone's got to stop this thing, and as you just saw, I have some power on my side. I see things differently because of that, too."

The L.T. saluted me and said, "Lieutenant MacPherson, reporting for duty, ma'am!"

Phil, in his Star Trooper armor, raised a hand. "I'm with you, Skye. Who else is with us?"

All hands went up. Even the biker girl who'd called me out raised his hand.

After all the lectures about my bad decisions, it was all I could do to keep tears from flowing again. *Not in front of everyone, not now.* My voice cracked as I said, "Thank you for the vote of confidence."

I walked up to the biker girl and said, "And thanks for speaking up. I'm not always right, and I need you to speak up if you think I'm wrong, okay?" She nodded.

I said to the crowd, "That goes for everyone. I might see things different, but that's no reason for blind trust. I'm not going to lie, that troll is bigger than a dump truck and twice as strong, older than the Liberty Bell and probably smarter than any of us. His soldiers might look like football players, but they're made of living rock, just like he is. One thing you should know, though. They're all vulnerable to iron. It burns them like it's white hot. So, some of your weapons will work better than others. Anyone got any ideas?"

My new favorite vampire role-player spoke up. "Well, I volunteer at the Real Adventure area, and we have nail guns to put together the sets."

"Don't those have to be plugged in?" said the L.T.

"Some of them, but we have a couple of cordless ones. I could run and get them?"

I smiled at her. "I hope there aren't any hard feelings between us, Raven. You know, at Heath's?"

She smiled back. "No, I don't really remember much from Heath's to be honest. But Raven's my vampire name, my real name—"

"Thanks, Raven. Take a couple others with you to gather any other tools that might be helpful."

They took off toward another side of the building with Ham and his crowbar as escort. The rest stood around talking about which weapons might be better than others. I offered advice, and as a double sort of test, touched a few myself. The nails tingled on my skin, the tire tools and crowbars made my skin crawl. Some of the older knives made me jerk my hand away; some of the "better quality" steel had no effect at all on my skin.

The L.T. approached me after a few minutes. "It'd be better if we knew more about what we're getting into in there, Skye. Some tactical advantage, maybe, or warning of an ambush?"

I wished for my Minnie right then, but had another idea.

"I'm going to sit down for a few minutes, okay? And I'm going to look asleep or dead maybe, but you've got to leave me be for a bit. I'm going to do some otherworldly spying."

"Huh?" said the L.T.

Phil walked up just then and said, "I think I know what she means. Astral projection, Skye? I thought that was Frannie's thing."

"Yeah, it is, and usually I can't, but these are special circumstances."

Phil nodded. "Okay, Skye. But it's scary. Frannie seemed dead for sure earlier today. I'm gonna try to wake you up if you're gone more than five minutes, okay?"

Earlier today? Wow, what a day. "Call it ten and you've got a deal," I said.

Phil nodded. I swept away glass on the ground near the building with my boot, and sat on the sidewalk. I leaned against the wall, not knowing what my body might do without me in it. My stomach clenched at that thought.

Crashes and booms sounded from inside, and I heard sirens approaching.

Not much time, Skye, better get to it. My hand found the amulet in my pocket, and I pulled it out. I had a sudden desire to keep it secret, so both hands covered it in my lap. Phil hovered nearby, and a few people in my army watched me.

"Phil, could you tell the troops I'm okay?"

He nodded. "You got it. Be careful. Come back, okay?"

I closed my eyes and took in a breath and let it out. Then, I concentrated on the amulet. I pictured standing up without my body.

I opened my eyes. I stood, Phil and the L.T. near me, and nothing seemed different. *Well crap, it didn't work!*

I almost tripped over some girl's long legs. Then I realized her boots looked exactly like mine. *Oh wow, super freaky!*

I marveled at the perspective, standing over myself like this. I hadn't realized how much tunnel mud and sewer grime I'd gotten on me. My jeans were streaked, my arms smudged. My head bowed, stringy hair framed my face. Asleep, or whatever I was, I looked peaceful. *That's what they say about dead people, isn't it?*

I found it too disturbing to look at myself like this, and felt the pressure of time. Also, the amulet could be taken from me at any time with nobody home inside.

I took a step and would have bumped into the L.T. if I hadn't passed right through him instead.

"Oops! Sorry!" I said, though the L.T. gave no sign he heard.

I expected the creepy cold spaghetti sensation I'd had when I'd phased into the fairy realm earlier. Instead, it tickled anyplace our bodies overlapped, and for a moment, I saw through the L.T.'s eyes. My beard itched and I had to pee and my leg ached from where I wiped out on the bike. Memories floated up, too confusing to sort out. Only one mattered at the moment; the memory of the giant troll as it burst from the Soldiers and Sailors Monument and kicked a few motorcycles and riders out of its way. That's when I wiped out.

The moment ended as I broke contact with the L.T. As I re-oriented myself, I watched as he shivered and looked around, eyes wild.

I avoided walking through Phil and a vampire gamer girl who wandered across my path before I entered the gaping hole where the doors had been.

I stopped in my tracks as the tether that connected me to my body pulled me up short. I peered over my shoulder and saw the silvery cable quiver with tension. *This isn't doing much good.*

Straining against it proved uncomfortable, but fruitless. Frustrated, I wished I could just reel it out like a retractable extension cord. A chill shiver covered me, and the cord fell slack, and I found my leash could pay out. How far, I had no idea, but I entered the convention center step by silent step.

The food court had been ransacked. Tables lay overturned or broken, chairs scattered everywhere. Piles of wrappers, Styrofoam packaging, and other garbage surrounded rooted out trash bins. Glass cases that once displayed pizza and sandwiches had been smashed in.

A shadow detached itself from the dark recesses of the food court and moved toward me. A short, pudgy shadow, with a gait so familiar I rushed forward.

"Stuart! Oh my God, is that you?" My voice sounded hollow to my ears, as though I spoke through a coffee can.

The shadow resolved into Stuart's features, and he smiled, standing a few feet away. "Hey hot stuff. We'd best make this visit short."

I put a fist on one hip and strutted up to him, playing a game we had in life, pretending to lord my height over him. It was my big guns; I knew it'd make him squirm. "Short, you say?"

He looked up at me and grinned. "Yeah, yeah. I can't even get a break in the afterlife, eh Skye?"

I hugged him to me and smooshed his face into my boobs. It pleased me that I *could* touch him, that we didn't pass right through each other.

"Okay Skye, this is fun, but I meant it, this has to be quick."

I sighed. "Damn it, why can't this be one of those things like a dream, where an hour is just a minute in the real world. It's been a hard couple of days. Annabelle dumped me, Stewie. Guess I'm a single girl again."

He pushed us apart enough to catch my eyes with his. He shook his head. "Nah. Never happened."

I nodded. "Yeah, it did. She had enough of my crap and cut me loose."

He shrugged. "She might say so, but don't make the same mistake you did with me. Don't give up too easy, Skye. Maybe today's not the day, maybe next week will be too soon, but let her come to you."

"You're awful helpful for a dead boyfriend. Are you trying to get rid of me?" I pouted. He can't resist the pout.

He grinned and struggled free of me. "You're alive, and I'm beyond worldly cares, Skye. Now, I gotta tell you, I know how you're here. And though I loved that kiss you laid on your friend yesterday, I'm here to warn you. Using the mojo that took over Ernie is bad news. Like Gollum and the One Ring bad news. I can *feel* it over there, pulsing with shadow energies. It's sucking out your life, Skye, and it's going to get you to suck the life out of your friends and enemies. It doesn't care. It's just a thing someone made."

"You're wrong. It does what I tell it to do."

He gave me a lopsided smile. "Maybe. But each thing you ask for *costs*, Skye. You could go Godzilla on the troll's ass with that, sure. But that'd take more wattage than your soul has in its battery. Maybe more than all the souls in your little army."

"I can handle it," I said.

He shook his head. "Yeah, that's what you think now. But the more you sip from this cup of power, the thirstier you'll get. You've never really been all that good at knowing when to stop."

I glared at him. "What's that supposed to mean?"

"You know I'm telling the truth, even if it hurts to hear it. This is strong stuff, and as you use it, you grow weaker. Stop using the shadow mojo right now while you can, Skye."

I always hated when Stuart was right. "Okay. I'll try not to use it unless I have to. Right now, I have to use it to go see what the Chained Lord is up to, so I don't lead those people out there into a trap."

He grinned. "If only you had an intangible friend to help you out there."

I laughed. "Okay, smart guy, what can you tell me?"

"I've been snooping around since we talked, and I watched as the trolls crashed in here. 'Course I don't see 'em all as trolls, but I don't need to see through glamours to figure it out, with the big guy crashing around like a pug romping through my action figure collection. It's totally a trap. He left this path for you, and others, to follow. He's all set up in there, like this big target, waiting for you, only a couple of guards nearby. The rest are camped out in the hall that intersects halfway down. They'll cut you off before you get anywhere near him."

"Well crap. I've got to get close to him, or all those other trolls are going to overwhelm me and the others."

He nodded. "If I were you? I'd go in some back way, in through the dealer room, and out the middle doors. You'll be right there, next to the stage, up his nose."

I grabbed him and planted a kiss on him, this time without Frannie acting as medium. Our spectral lips touched and maybe it was just the memory of our flesh on flesh, but it sure felt real to me. He kissed back, and for a long moment, nothing else mattered.

We locked gazes afterward, and he smiled and whispered, "You better go. Meter's running, and you can't afford the cab fare. See ya around."

"How?"

He shrugged. "We'll figure something else out. But life is for the living, and I mean it when I wish you and your girlfriend the best. I just want you to be happy, and I'll catch you on the flip side."

"I love you too, Stuart." But before I could say more, he faded out like a ghost.

Well, exactly *like a ghost.*

Chapter Twenty-Four

I reeled in my cord, followed it back to where my body sat slumped. I watched as Phil and the L.T. fussed over me, poking and slapping at my cheeks. Phil called my name and the L.T. cursed.

I shouted at them. "Hey! That's me! Cut that out! I'm going to slap you!"

Either their slapping had an effect or "I'm going to slap you" is the magic phrase that ends astral projection into the shadow world, because my point of view snapped from third person to first.

Phil's slap stung. I snapped my eyes open and blocked his hand with my arm before he could land another one. "Damn it, Phil, stop!"

The L.T. poked me once more in the shoulder, but I startled Phil so bad that he stumbled and fell, landing both of them in a heap next to me. The Star Trooper armor made an awful crunching noise on the bits of glass on the sidewalk under Phil's butt.

"S-skye! You're alive!" cried Phil.

"Shit, girl, you quit breathing! Phil wanted to call 911," said the L.T., dragging himself to a crouch to peer at me with wide eyes.

Like a turtle on its back, Phil still struggled to get up, hampered by his bulk and his armor.

I had pins and needles all over my body as I pushed myself up and offered a hand to help Phil up. "They'd probably laugh at you. I think most of the ambulances in the city are still on the circle."

"Yeah," said the L.T., grabbing Phil's other hand. We heaved together and all three of us stood up. "Not to mention, Homeland Security's here, and if we hadn't gotten here first, we'd be shut out."

"About that. We have to find another way in. A back way."

Ham and the two vampire gamers arrived, carrying four cases and a canvas bag. They grinned, and Raven held a yellow nail gun with a hefty battery pack. She said "Ka-pow! Ka-pow!" and gestured with the power tool like an actual gun.

"Hey," I said, "You guys know any other way in?"

Raven said, "Yeah, we went through the loading dock out back."

Flashing lights of emergency vehicles came into view. "Ham, I need you to stay here to lead a big diversion. We can't let the Chained Lord know we're up to something. We'll take one of the nail guns. You keep the rest. You're gonna need them, I think. I'll take these gamers and the L.T. and head around back. When you hear fighting inside, I need you to rush in and attack. I'll have their attention, so you'll get in some free shots. Then make a fighting retreat, okay? Ignore what happens to me, I need you to draw out as many of them as you can. And try not to get hurt!"

Phil stepped up and joined the vamp party.

I shook my head. "No. You don't have a weapon and that armor won't help you against these trolls."

Phil frowned. "I think this is a bad idea, Skye."

I kept anger out of my voice as best I could. "And that's why I need you to stay here. I need you to believe in me and my ideas. It's on me to fix this as best I can, Phil. Stay here. You're the only one who knows Rebecca of this bunch. If you see her, tell her I'm going to need a path to get out."

"But—"

"Got it?"

Phil nodded, sullen.

"Okay Raven, let's go," I said, plucking the sleeves of the L.T. and a couple other vampire gamers as I followed her toward the back of the convention center, the others in tow.

As we hustled along, I heard a voice bark something unintelligible over a bullhorn. I hoped my crew could hold fast. No damage showed on this side of the building. I took it as a good sign that the Chained Lord expected me to do the reckless thing and make a frontal assault.

Instead of the reckless thing I'm actually doing.

I'm going to stop right here and admit I wished I had my flask, or a Heath brew, *anything* alcoholic right then. My nerves were jangled and I wished I had some spy support from Minnie. Not to mention the prospect of going up against a ten ton troll and his army of rock-headed minions filled me with a chilling terror. Meanwhile, the amulet in my pocket offered a seductive source of power that might have to be my last resort, if everyone turned out to be right about my bad choices. I could always tap that and turn the tide, right?

Stuart's warning rang in my ears, and I knew I couldn't walk away from that without being owned like Ernie had. Without losing everything that made me Skye.

We rounded a corner and ran down a ways more until we got to the convention center loading docks. I saw a dozen or more massive garage-type doors lined the back of the building, semi trailers backed up to many of them. Raven led us past six or seven closed loading dock doors to one that stood open a couple of inches. She clambered up the chest-high dock and pushed. The door rolled up a couple of feet and she ducked under.

The L.T. looked skeptical. "Won't it go higher?"

Raven stuck her head out from under the door, and said, "Not unless you want me to try the hydraulics. Dunno what kind of hearing those guys have."

I shrugged. "You're right, running as quiet as we can would be best."

The L.T. made a step out of his hands and I let him hoist me up. I helped a couple other vampire gamers up as he did them the same favor. Last of all, the L.T. refused help, trying to be macho. It took a couple of tries, and Raven and I ended up just hauling him up.

The gamers had to break out phones to use as flashlights in the dark of the dock. Raven unpacked the nail gun from its case and fed a belt of nails into its slot. She favored me with a maniacal grin.

I smiled. "Don't let that thing go off before we need it, but keep it ready. If he's set guards or patrols, we can't lose our element of surprise."

She nodded and said, "This is where Real Adventure's stuff was unloaded a few days ago. There's some crates over here that had the set structure pieces. I think there's galvanized steel pipe in there. Is that iron enough?"

She led me to a big wooden crate and handed me a heavy pipe. It tingled a bit in my grasp. *The wonderbooze has long worn off, why do I keep feeling aftereffects?*

I nodded and handed out pipes to the L.T. and the other vampire gamers. "Yeah, this will have some effect on the trolls. Not devastating, but better than nothing for sure."

And you know? I still missed that silly wrought iron fireplace poker. It had bought me some healthy respect from the fairy folk. Or at least it put fear in them.

We left the loading dock bay and filed into an access corridor, lit far brighter that was comfortable for me. We squinted at each other for a few moments as our eyes adjusted, and then Raven led the way. The interior corridors were like another world alongside the world of Big Con, interwoven with the rest of the convention center, but hidden. Raven led us into the dealer hall, which had lights dimmed down to a dull orange twilight, just enough not to run into things. Eerie and indistinct in this light, booths and displays loomed up to menace us as we approached.

Rounding the corner of a Styrofoam castle, a troll stood at least two Skyes tall, one heavy clawed hand raised up to swat us like bugs.

I whipped out the Fairy Hilt. I'd lost all my buzz but could still see a faint outline of the blade. The troll held its pose, and I felt my skin prickle, waiting for that hand to fall on me. I drew back my arm to strike off its head to keep it from calling out, then swung.

Nothing happened. The troll stood still, unharmed.

KERCHUNK.

Raven hit the troll with the nail gun.

Nothing happened.

The L.T. rushed up and put a hand on my shoulder and held back Raven with his other hand. "Hold up there, ladies. You're attacking a statue."

Gamer phone lights focused on the detailed sculpture painted and shaped so much like a troll that I still had a doubt for a moment whether the L.T. guessed right. It stood still, and its black hole eyes stared out past us.

Freaking Big Con. What a relief.

"So much for quiet," said the L.T.

I held a finger to my lips and motioned everyone into a booth. We all hunkered down and listened for a long minute.

The distant clamor of a crowd reached my ears, a kettledrum voice answered by raucous applause. Raven started to rise, but the L.T. shook his head, and she stayed in a crouch.

An awful thought came to me. *What if there are things I can't see here? Like those tiny gargoyles at Heath's, or other fairy types like Minnie, whose glamour makes them invisible?*

"Hey L.T.," I said.

"Yeah?"

"If you have a flask on you, I'd be in your debt for a shot."

He shook his head. "I'm out, sorry Skye."

I sighed. "Probably best anyway."

None of us heard any sounds inside the immense space of the dealer hall, just the troll party going on outside. After a few beats longer than necessary, I stood and motioned for the others to follow me. We wove around endless displays of dice, stacks of board games up to my chest, T-shirt walls that reached up a couple of stories high, past dioramas so intricate I felt like a giant, and up to the bank of doors under an EXIT sign in the center of that quarter-mile long hall's far wall.

The noise, especially the Chained Lord's speech, increased in volume as we approached. The doors shook.

This is it, Skye, it's show time.

"Okay, we're going to burst out into the hall and you guys have to clear a path for me to run up to the Chained Lord and whack him."

"Got it," said the L.T.

Raven checked the nail gun's switch and gave me thumbs up. The others hefted their galvanized steel pipes.

That's when the doors opened.

We stood there, caught flat-footed, as Obsidian and Brick each held a door, revealing us to a crowd of trolls, surrounding the dais that Ernie and I had occupied earlier that night.

THUD-CRACK! THUD-CRACK!

Their king stepped into view, chains dangling from manacles, a broad smile upon his jagged, milky quartz face. "Hoh ah ah, you shouldn't keep me waiting like that, fairykin. Let's talk

about what you have, what I want, and why you will give it to me, hmmm?"

Like hell I will! I drew the Fairy Hilt and crouched. The blade might have been made of glass for all I could see it while sober. But I drew in a breath and readied myself for an all-out attack on the troll king.

Limestone stepped from behind the Chained Lord, carrying a bundle. The bundle wriggled, and I saw it was a person, wrapped in a mile of rope, mouth gagged with a cloth tied around her head, red hair draped around her wild eyes and chubby cheeks.

The Chained Lord reached for the bundle and stroked the length of her bound body with one arm-thick finger, ending the gesture under her chin. "I do hope we can be civilized about this."

Chapter Twenty-Five

I stood there, frozen, unable to think. One of the vampires dropped his iron pipe and fled back into the dealer room.

Holy crap! I can't attack, he'll kill Frannie! But I can't back down now, either. Better stall for time to think. "Something you wanted? But I already *gave* you your freedom. And you gave me Minnie, and we shared a drink. Seems to me we're even-Steven. Right big guy?"

Everyone stood still as a freeze-frame. The floor groaned as the Chained Lord shifted his weight from foot to foot. "Hoh. Brave little thing, joking while a single word from me, a single wrong move from you and your friend's head will be twisted off, snick-snap. And then, my army will grind you into strawberry jam, magic sword or no."

Just then, I heard a voice in my head. Stuart's whispered voice. "Skye, think about what he is and what he wants. Fire and ice, Skye. To win, you've got to lose. You've got to lose, Skye!"

I tried to reply with unspoken words in my head. *Stuart! That makes no sense at all!*

The Chained Lord growled and the floor under my feet trembled. At least, I think it was the floor.

How can I 'hold fast' and lose at the same time?

"How about if I hand it over to you, you'll just go back and rule the underground, like Bask rules the transit lines? We'll have a deal, and everyone's happy! Win-win!" I showed him my teeth and hoped it looked like a smile, not a threat.

The Chained Lord stared at me, eyes hooded in inky recesses under his brows. He raised a hand above his head, dragging the iron chain up, then drove his fist down on the floor with an ear-splitting boom. "No! There will be no more deals. You bear the mark of an Oathbreaker. I can take what I want, or you can give it to me. I may show mercy, if you are quick about it."

Crap. Now I'm marked? Hold fast… fire and ice… I can't fight, I can't flee… I guess that leaves—
KER-CHUNK!

I whirled and saw that Raven had rushed forward and nailed Obsidian with the gun. Cracks formed in his body. His scream filled the air like a chandelier crashing to the floor. The cracks widened and spread. Then, Obsidian flew apart and became nothing but a pile of rubble.

A wave of nausea washed over me. As much as I disliked the little tyrant, I hadn't expected the nail gun to be quite so *effective*.

A silence echoed off the walls for a heartbeat or two. Raven's nervous laughter broke the silence and my eyes locked with Raven's for a split second. In them, Raven's triumph melted and new terror ignited.

At the same time, her stupid act of defiance lit a different kind of fire in me. I raised my family's blade to point at the Chained Lord's belly. I stared into those black hole eyes and to the L.T. and Raven I said, "Hold your positions. Hold fast."

The Chained Lord roared and his army roared with him. The first ranks, several dozen strong, advanced, approaching from behind their king.

I glanced at Limestone, who had not harmed Frannie. He stood frozen, awaiting orders. I had just a little time to act. *I guess everyone expected* me *to be the one to do something stupid first. So, time to get stupid.*

While my friends held the doors, I sprinted up the dais, the point of my sword always trained on the giant troll's belly. All I could think of in that moment was a cartoon I'd seen on the internet of an eagle about to grab a mouse up in its talons, while the mouse gave it the finger. *A last act of defiance!*

I stuck my hand in my pocket and pulled out the amulet. The cold tingling crawled up my arm and a sudden desire flooded through me, an image of using the amulet's power to grow to giant size or to conquer the troll's mind like Ernie had enslaved all those people. *I would be their Queen, and they would say my name with awe. They'd cry out, Skye! Skye! Skye!*

Like a thousand zombies had earlier today, in this very room. Mindless and obedient.

The craving for that power weakened my will. I *wanted* to rule these monsters. I'd save the day, I'd be a hero, and Rebecca couldn't deny it. My power would turn Annabelle's heart, and she would believe in me again. *Skye! Skye! Skye!*

A smile pulled at my lips. The smile parted my lips, baring my teeth in a grin. A threat, this time.

The Chained Lord hesitated and drew back, just a fraction. *He knows I have the upper hand, even now.*

More kerchunks echoed through the hall along with screams and other sounds of battle. *My army! Oh crap, they can't get killed, please don't let them get killed!*

"Your friend dies, fairykin. Now."

And Limestone raised Frannie over his head and she screamed. I saw wild panic in her eyes, and a flash of Gonzo on the gurney came to me, his words came to me again, "Do what you gotta."

And then it hit me. I knew exactly what I had to do. *Fire and ice!*

I fought back the cold fire of the amulet's seductive power and lowered my blade. I held the amulet out to the Chained Lord. "Take it. It's yours."

"HALT!" cried the troll king. The army stopped, just behind him. He held out a hand, and I dropped the amulet into a palm big enough to crush me where I stood.

"MINE!" The Chained Lord clenched his fingers into a fist, surrounding the shadow amulet. He raised the fist to punch the ceiling. His army cheered. I peered at Limestone and watched as he set Frannie to the ground to free his hands to beat them together while he chanted along with the others. "Lord of trolls! Lord of trolls! Lord of trolls!"

I bounded down the dais stairs and caught the L.T.'s eye and pointed to Frannie. He nodded and ran up and bashed Limestone with his metal pipe. Limestone doubled over and hit the ground like an avalanche. The L.T. unsheathed a knife from his boot and slashed at the ropes holding Frannie.

In my peripheral vision, Raven turned another nearby troll to gravel with her nail gun. KER-CHUNK!

I slashed at the Chained Lord's belly with my sword, and he roared and brought down his fist. Speed or luck saved me from the pile driver blow he dealt the floor, though the concussion knocked me from my feet. As I sprawled, something hot and wet trickled down my arm. *Blood? Am I bleeding? Am I cut?*

The troll king raised his fist to bash at me again, but stopped as thick, viscous liquid dribbled from his fist. Bits of rock flaked off, revealing a massive fist of flesh under the stone. The crumbling continued, like a fast-motion consuming disease. His granite skin cracked and broke, exposing hairy ashen flesh underneath. The manacle hung loose on his wrist and all either of us could do was stare as the crumbling revealed his new flesh-and-blood arm and spread over his shoulder and up his neck and across his chest.

The Chained Lord bellowed. His voice changed from a deep earthy rumble to a fleshy, elephant-like trumpet. His advancing troops stopped and backed up, forming a wider circle around him, perhaps in case it was contagious.

Fire and ice! Stuart, I love you! A commotion broke out behind the widening circle, more kerchunks and shouting drawing nearer and nearer. The line of trolls had grown so thin I could see my army fighting their way toward us from the doors to the street. I scrambled to my feet and shouted at the L.T., who half-carried a dazed-looking Frannie, and Raven. "Go! Now!"

Raven rushed ahead and threatened the trolls in her way with the nail gun. They fell back, and a couple of Star Troopers with nail guns burst through, dividing the mass of trolls into two groups. Raven cheered and jumped up and down.

I shouldn't have been watching her; I should have been covering our retreat. I'd been so focused on getting the hell away from the Chained Lord as he transmuted from stone to flesh that I thought he wasn't a threat. If I could go back and do it over again, this is my biggest regret, since I haven't got an excuse for it. Not "drunk Skye couldn't concentrate" or "terrified Skye couldn't act" or "Skye couldn't do anything against a foe so terrible." No, I had the Hilt, I was sober, and I had far too much adrenaline pumping through me for fear to grip my brain.

I just screwed up.

The Chained Lord swung an arm and his immense iron chain whipped past my feet and flipped into the air and wrapped around Raven. He jerked on the chain and she bent in half like a rag doll in a dog's jaws, and flew toward him.

She died instantly, her neck broken. I tell myself when I replay this scene over and over in my head. I hope it was true. Her head did snap back at an unnatural angle. Before he grabbed up her limp body and bit her in two.

My volunteer army screamed and ran. I ran after them, terror catching up to me. All rational thought shredded in the blender of my panicked mind. *It's all my fault! All my fault!*

The trolls closed in, and the L.T., burdened by Frannie, slowed my flight. I caught up to him and he turned to me and said, "Slow them down, Skye, or we're all dead." His eyes burned with something I hadn't seen in him before, a kind of hot determination. His jaw muscles bulged as he clamped down his teeth and redoubled his efforts to drag Frannie through the narrowing gap of trolls.

His words hit me like a bucket of cold water and I turned and brandished the Hilt. My terror turned to rage, and the intangible magic sword blazed to life, no longer a faint outline to my eyes, but a solid bar of flaming blue light. I slashed in a wild arc around me, forcing the nearby trolls to back off.

The Chained Lord stepped from the rubble that had fallen away from his new body, dropping the rest of Raven to the ground. His eyeballs rolled within their sockets, then fixed on me and narrowed. "MacLeod! What did you do to me? What did you do?"

I backed up as I talked, guiding my retreat by the sound of my fleeing volunteers. I can't tell you how much I wanted to bolt and follow them as fast as my legs would carry me. *Hold fast, Skye, hold fast, hold fast!*

My mouth dry, I said, hoping it came out as more than a squeak, "You did it yourself. You took the shadow into you."

He followed my retreat, step by slow step. He stayed out of sword-range, for now. Those eyes as big as volleyballs made my stomach shrink into a cold knot, almost preferring the glowing coals he'd had before he'd transformed.

"I am the troll king! I am older than this city! I forged this when your people lived across the ocean! How can this be?"

I had no idea, but I needed time. I've learned a trick or two from Bask, so I made something up. "It's changed since you made it. It's tapped into power you never meant it to have. It's had time to grow, even as you've sat underground for all that time, stagnant.

It's used people, become a conduit that grants wishes and steals souls. You're not of this world, and it's a black hole to another. Fire and ice, troll king, they don't mix. Fairy and shadow magic canceled each other out, and you're not really a troll anymore. 'Cause you're not part of the fairy world anymore, and you're not part of the shadow world, either. You're a creature of *my* world now."

He roared and slammed his bloody fist into the floor between us. The floor shook but his face contorted. *Is that pain I see?* "No, it can't be true."

I bumped into the L.T.'s back and almost tripped, but I recovered and swung the Hilt around in another wide arc to get the trolls away, to make a bigger pathway.

The Chained Lord lagged behind me, and I needed him to follow me.

"How else can you explain it? Do I *look* like I know how to cast spells that can turn a giant ancient troll into a real boy? Think I have a sorcerer in my jeans pocket, maybe? I'm just a girl with a magic sword, and all I did was give you what you asked for, you colossal dick!"

He screamed in rage and swung his chain at me. The Hilt's blade flamed up as it sliced through the iron and I ducked down as the severed piece flew end over end over me. A sizzle and a howl caused me to look, and I saw an earthen troll on the ground, a chain-shaped brand across its body, the iron links in a pile nearby. The trolls backed away.

I cried, "L.T.! You good?" I kept my eyes on the Chained Lord, who swiped at my feet with the chain on his other arm. I'd skipped a lot of rope as a girl, so it passed under me. I chopped at that chain, too, and another section skittered off. Trolls on the other side crashed into each other to avoid the iron.

"Almost there, Highlander!"

"Only Gonzo gets to call me that!"

"Whatever!"

My boots crunched glass underfoot and the night air caressed my sweaty face. The troll king had to duck as he followed me outside.

"I may be flesh now, fairykin, but I'll outlast you all the same. And when you falter, I will pull you apart and show you your insides before you die."

I stood in the middle of Capitol Avenue. Sirens wailed, lights of various emergency colors flashed all around. A helicopter hovered far above, and the Chained Lord stood before me, silhouetted by its spotlight.

A large engine revved somewhere up the street. I took a swipe at the Chained Lord with my sword and drew a horizontal line of blood across his belly.

A voice whispered in my ear. *Jump, lassie!*

"I'd be glad to test that theory, but I've got to catch a bus," I said, and dove to the side.

The Chained Lord only had time to half-turn to watch me before an IndyGo bus plowed into him at highway speed.

Chapter Twenty-Six

Time slowed almost to a stop. Meat and metal heaped before me, lit by the wild flashing emergency lights. I smelled gasoline and yelled for everyone to back up. I sprung from the ground and ran, but it was as though my feet slogged through a foot of mud. I had more than enough time to notice the more or less intact back end of the bus, whose display read "TERMINAL."

My memory may be wrong, but I'd swear the wave of heat of the fire hit me before the light or sound. No concussion followed, just a terrible stink of burning gas, vinyl from the seats, hair, and flesh.

I ran until hands caught me and stopped me. EMTs in scrubs looked me over with wide, scared eyes. I shook my head and waved them off and sat down on a curb to catch my breath. I closed my eyes and shook.

A small person sat next to me. A little hand touched my shoulder. "Ye did good, lassie."

I kept my eyes closed and said nothing for awhile. His hand slid away. I reached out and took it in mine. Small though it might be, his hand held on tight as I shook with sobs of relief and grief.

"It's all my fault," I said.

"Mebbe, mebbe not, lass. The past is done, an' whether ye made a mistake in it does nae matter. What matters is how ye fix it. Ye did good, and that's important, eh?"

I shrugged. He squeezed my hand.

"Why'd you help me? You said I'm an Oathbreaker."

"Aye, that ye are, lass. That means I can nae take your word. It does nae mean I give up on ye."

"I guess."

"Plus, there was a great fat monster stompin' around me city, I could nae have that, eh?"

I laughed. "Right, can't have that." I opened my eyes and looked at him. The merry glint in his eye seemed at total odds with the wreckage, smoke and stink around us. The sparkle, lit by flames behind me, held no malice, only a mix of amusement and concern.

"Bask, I want to apologize."

He shrugged.

"I'm sorry. Maybe if I'd kept my word and given you the amulet, you could have stopped the Chained Lord in some less messy way. Maybe Raven would be alive now."

He shrugged and held my gaze with a steady, serious look. "Mebbe. Or mebbe you'd have two monsters ta defeat. If th' shadow bauble did that to a great ancient troll king, what might it do to a wee guide of the straight tracks like me?"

I smiled. "Don't bullshit me, T.K. I know you're no pushover."

He shook his head. "That I'm not. I've got me a knight in denim armor at my side, straight out of the MacLeod legends. Ye bested an ancient monster, an' rid the world of a nasty bit o' shadow magic in one go."

"Shut up," I said and let go his hand. I watched as firefighters worked on the blaze. I searched for a petite suited figure, but didn't find one. "You're the one who had the guts to drive a bus into a two-story troll. How'd you survive that one?"

"Ye think I stayed at the wheel the whole way? Nae, I popped out about the time ye jumped out from behind the troll."

I nodded. "Fairy magic again, right."

He shrugged. "Beats makin' cookies in a great big tree, hmm?"

I didn't want to laugh, but I did.

I said, "So where do we go from here?"

"Up to you, lass," he said, watching me.

I held the Hilt out to him, point down. "In place of the favor, would you take this? I want things to be good between us. I don't want to be an Oathbreaker."

The whites of the old gnome's eyes showed. "Ye can nae be serious, lass. I can nae take yer family's greatest treasure."

"We're kin, you said so yourself. Take it."

He put his hand on the Hilt above mine. I let go. It seemed it should be too heavy for him to easily wield, but he held it out in front of him with wonder in his eyes. "Lass. I can nae take it. Not forever. How about I hold on ta it, as guardian, an' I let ye have it in times o' need?"

"Yeah, sure, that works for me. I'm not sure I ought to be doing this hero stuff anymore."

He laughed and clapped a hand on my back. "Lass, there's no one better suited than ye fer this sort o' thing."

I shook my head. "No, I'm a terrible hero. I have to drink to be effective, and if I drink too much, I screw things up so badly, it's better I never did anything at all."

He smiled, eyes crinkling at the corners. "Skye, ye have ta know, age has a lot ta do with it. Yer young, even by yer own standards. Still findin' yer own path. No hero hatches from an egg fully formed, eh?"

"Yeah? I didn't listen to you or to Rebecca, and what happened? Ernie enslaved thousands of people, I let Trollzilla loose, Gonzo and dozens of other bikers got hurt, Ernie got shot, and Raven's *dead*."

His brow furrowed and his eyes glared. "An' had ye listened, Ernie still would ha' gotten an army together, an' the troll woulda eaten him ta get the amulet, an' he would still have stomped aroun' my city like a rubber suited monster. Mebbe it woulda been worse. Mebbe yer ol' Transit King woulda bit it tryin' ta stop him, hmm? Mebbe yer girlfriend too? Mebbe a lot more woulda died, Skye. Stop bein' hard on yerself fer tryin' ta do good. Ye held fast ta what ye thought was right, and ye put others before ye. Always easiest ta look back on yer mistakes after ye've made 'em. Not so easy lookin' forward."

"What good is a superhero who's afraid to use her superpower? I can't keep drinking my way through life. I can't hold a job, and I make bad choices when lives are at stake."

His eyes focused on me, looked into me, and he smiled. "How many trolls did ye see in the great hall?"

I shrugged. "Dozens. A hundred, maybe."

He nodded. "An' how drunk were ye?"

"I… I was sober by then."

His face split in a grin. "See?"

I shook my head. "See what?"

He snapped his fingers in front of my face. "Ye great dunce! Ye saw through troll glamour without any booze! Mebbe ye don't need it after all!"

Oh! "Really? But there are so many times I can't, how's that work then?"

He shrugged and stood, a grin still on his face. Standing, his face was level with mine as I sat there on the curb. "I can nae solve all yer riddles, Skye, but now ye've got a puzzler ta work on, hmm?"

And then the little guy hugged me. I hugged him back and cried on him for a minute.

I let go and wiped at my tears, embarrassed.

When I looked up, he was gone.

A few feet away stood a somewhat taller figure, her face darkened by soot, her eyes bright, and her chapped lips parted to speak. "Hey, Skye."

"Annabelle—"

She reached a hand out and put a finger across my lips. She said, "Don't speak, not yet. I need to say I'm sorry. I mean, I'm still upset and confused, and I don't know what to do next, so I'm not sorry I told you how I felt. But I'm sorry it had to come out like that, back there."

I curled my fingers around the one she had on my lips. I kissed her finger, and then took her hand in mine. I waited for her to go on, afraid to meet her eyes, but dared to anyway. I stood up, and she tilted her head back to look up at me. Sometimes I'm not so fond of being tall. S*he ought to be towering over me, not the other way around.*

She said, "Skye, I meant how I felt, but I didn't mean it when I said I wanted you to go away. I want you in my life. I need you."

"I need you too, Belle. You have no idea."

She closed her eyes a moment, took a breath, and then opened them. "I'm tired of besing the grownup. It's overrated. I hate hearing myself nag you, I hate that I resent you when bad things happen, because I have to be the one to be responsible in the real world while you have one foot in the fairy world. I mean, I know it's real, too, but we have to have a place to live, we have to have money to eat."

"I know, Belle, and I'm sorry I've put you in that position. You're not my mommy. You're my love. And it's hard for me. If I'm sober, I'm afraid of the monsters that I know are all around us, unseen unless I have a drink. But I screw up when I drink too much, and in the heat of the action, I don't know how much is enough and how much is too much. And I miss a part of me when I go without; I can't talk to my Minnie."

She nodded, and her eyes shined in the flashing lights of the nearby emergency vehicles.

"Belle, I'm going to quit for awhile. No drinking. I'm going to work on using my second sight while sober."

"Skye, you don't have to—"

I nodded and put a finger across her lips. "Yes, I do. I need help, though. I want to show you that I can make good choices. It's long past time, Belle, I see that. I need to try."

She threw her arms around me, and we held each other in a tight hug. She smelled of smoke, and the burning, flashing, shouting world around us no longer mattered. I turned my head to look in her eyes, but she caught me in a kiss. Her parched lips locked with mine, and my heart soared and I forgot all about trolls, zombies, Big Con, death, and destruction for a long moment. We existed outside of our world, not in shadow, not in fairy, but in a world all our own. I could have stayed there forever.

"Hoody hoo, go Skye! No *wonder* you resisted the ol' L.T.'s charms!"

Annabelle and I jumped apart at the sudden close voice. I could have smacked the L.T. again, but I didn't this time.

"Jerk!" I said, smiling.

Annabelle was not amused. She put her hands on her hips and glared at Gonzo's biker friend. "Who's this asshole?"

The L.T. affected a wounded look.

I looked from one to the other. "Annabelle, meet the L.T., he helped me beat the troll, and he saved Frannie. Once you get past his sleazy act, he's a real teddy bear inside. L.T., allow me to introduce my girlfriend, Annabelle. Don't mess with her, she might look small, but she can kick even your Marine ass if you make her mad."

They looked each other up and down, appraising. The L.T. broke the silence first and stuck out a hand. "Pleased to meet you.

You've got a great gal there in Skye. I fought in Iraq and I haven't seen many braver."

She took his hand and shook it. "Thanks. I don't doubt it. She's very special to me."

I think I blushed. "Shut up, you're both so full of it."

They both laughed and I smiled.

The L.T. said, "Skye, about that. In war, sometimes people die. It's hard to be the one that lives on. Raven signed up for it, and she started the fight. She may not have deserved to die like that, but she bought us time to get away. She bought everyone time. Without her, you me, and Frannie at least would have bit it, drowning in trolls. Maybe everyone would have."

I shook my head and sighed.

"Frannie's just dazed, she's chilling out over there while they check her out. Gonzo's gonna be fine, too, the EMTs promised me. He'll be in a cast or two. We can write dirty words on them, right?"

I smiled for a second and looked up at him. "And Ernie?"

"Your bosslady came by and said he'd live. Told me to tell you thanks, but wouldn't say what for."

"She said she was my boss?"

"Yeah. Past tense. Said not to lose your phone, whatever that means."

I sighed, and fatigue sank deep into my bones. I wanted a drink, and felt a pang of loss when I remembered my promise. "Guess we'll see what happens."

Annabelle took my hand again and squeezed. "Yeah, I guess we will."

About the Author

E. Chris Garrison writes fantasy and science fiction novels and short stories.

Her urban fantasies feature ghosts, demonic possession, and sinister fairy folk delivered with a "lightly dark" side of humor.

Her latest series is Trans-Continental, a steampunk adventure with a transgender woman protagonist. The series is set in one of the worlds in Chris's dimension-hopping science fiction adventure, Reality Check, also published by Silly Hat Books. Reality Check reached #1 in Science Fiction on Amazon.com in 2013. Silly Hat Books released Alien Beer and Other Stories, a collection of her short stories, in 2017.

Chrissy lives in Indianapolis, Indiana, with her wife, step- daughter and many cats. She also enjoys gaming, home brewing beer, and finding innovative uses for duct tape. Keep up on the latest news and releases from Chris at https://sillyhatbooks.com/

Photo Credit: (c) Ellie Sophia Photography

www.elliesophia.com

This book is part of an author-cooperative urban fantasy universe. Characters created by E. Chris Garrison (including Skye MacLeod and the Transit King) and R.J. Sullivan (including "Blue" Shaefer and Rebecca Burton) interact in a shared world. For example, Chris's Transit King appears in R.J.'s Haunting Obsession, while R.J.'s Rebecca Burton lends a hand in Chris's Mean Spirit. So if you love what you just read and want the entire story, here's a handy guide and timeline to:

The Skye-Blue-niverse

Haunting Blue by R.J. Sullivan *
Four 'Til Late by E. Chris Garrison**
Haunting Obsession by R.J. Sullivan
Sinking Down by E. Chris Garrison**
Blue Spirit by E. Chris Garrison
Me and the Devil by E. Chris Garrison**
Virtual Blue by R.J. Sullivan*
Restless Spirit by E. Chris Garrison
Mean Spirit by E. Chris Garrison

*Also part of The Collected Adventures of Blue Shaefer by R.J. Sullivan
**Part of the Road Ghosts Omnibus by E. Chris Garrison

Enter the Skye-Blue-niverse at:

https://sillyhatbooks.com/
and
https://rjsullivanfiction.com/

9 781953 763211